———————— ★ ————————

Claire appeared in the center of the screen, just moments before the call came in. They all settled down to watch.

CLAIRE: You're on the air with Claire.

CALLER: It's your fault, you know?

CLAIRE (*laughing*): I—I'm sorry? What did you say?

CALLER: I said it's your fault they're dead.

CLAIRE: What?

CALLER: Are you shocked? That I blame you, Claire?

CLAIRE: Yes, I am. Why would you?

CALLER: Because you made me do it? You made me kill them.

CLAIRE: (*eyes darting about for a moment, then realizing she won't be getting any help*): Are you telling me that you killed those three women?

CALLER: With my own two hands.

CLAIRE: Then why is it my fault?

CALLER: You seduce people.

CLAIRE: What people?

CALLER: The women who watch you. You seduce them into buying things they don't need. I just called to tell you that even though I'm on to you, there won't be any more women killed.

CLAIRE: Well, that's a relief.

CALLER: Once you're dead, Claire!

Click!

———————— ★ ————————

MURDER
IS THE DEAL OF THE DAY

Robert Randisi
Christine Matthews

TORONTO • NEW YORK • LONDON
AMSTERDAM • PARIS • SYDNEY • HAMBURG
STOCKHOLM • ATHENS • TOKYO • MILAN
MADRID • WARSAW • BUDAPEST • AUCKLAND

MURDER IS THE DEAL OF THE DAY

A Worldwide Mystery/October 2003

First published by St. Martin's Press, Incorporated.

ISBN 0-373-26472-0

Printed in U.S.A.

With love to
Jan and
John & Barbara:
the reasons we came here,
the reasons we stay.

And for Marcus from his mother:
Thank you for inspiring me
with your exceptional talent and wisdom.

PROLOGUE

"…AND THIS IS our special deal of the day…" the woman on the TV screen said.

The man watching the television turned to the dead woman and asked, "What do you think of this broad?"

When she didn't answer, he turned away and continued watching. Using the VCR remote control, the killer froze Claire Hunt on the screen. He stared at her for a few moments, admiring her good looks, then rewound the tape. Yeah, she was a babe all right, but that didn't mean she was special; she could get hurt, just the same as everyone else. When it got to the beginning, he pressed the stop button but left the VCR and television set on. The red power light glowed. Even a cop would notice that.

He stood up from where he'd been sitting next to the dead woman on the sofa and put the remote control in her hand. Her eyes were open—he had seen to that— staring at the television in blind wonder.

"Sorry, honey, nothing personal, but you just happened to get caught in the middle of something."

ONE

CLAIRE HUNT UNHOOKED the miniature microphone from her blouse and dropped it on the counter.

"Claire," Harve Wilson, her director, said, rushing up to her, "I'm sorry the damn thing went out at such a bad time—"

"A bad time, Harve?" Claire asked. "How about the worst time?"

"I know, I know…"

"When do we get a new mike?"

Wilson shrugged. "I've talked to Mr. Thurman about it, Claire—"

"Well, talk to him again," Claire said, cutting the man off.

Harve Wilson was in his late forties and squat, what a generous person would call "homely." But he was a decent man, which is why Claire instantly felt sorry for snapping at him.

"Look, Harve," she said, putting her hand on the man's shoulder, "I know you're doing your best. Talk to Ben, tell him how important it is that we have a new mike for tomorrow's show."

"Okay, Claire—"

"Or I'm not going on."

"What? Wait—" Wilson shouted as Claire walked away.

Without slowing down, she spoke over her shoulder, "I don't think it's too much to ask."

"Claire…Claire!…I'll work on it, Claire…."

Claire waved without turning around and walked out of the studio.

TBN WAS A SMALL cable station based in St. Louis. Founded six years ago, it was now five times larger than it had been during its first year, which still made it one of the smaller cable stations in the country. Benjamin Thurman, the owner of the station, was a contradiction. A rich man who pulled out all the stops when it came to getting his television station up and running, but once it was operating, he tried not to spend any more money than was necessary. That was why Claire Hunt had to worry about things like microphones malfunctioning.

Two years ago, however, she'd had greater worries than a simple piece of equipment. She'd had to worry about surviving in an industry populated with hard young bodies. She'd had so many jobs in small-market TV stations that, without even realizing it, age and experience left her an on-air "personality." As she approached forty-two, it seemed no one wanted the "mature" woman she had become. She did get one offer to host a game show, but she was saved from accepting it when Ben Thurman approached her.

As she left the Grand Boulevard address where TBN had their studios, she checked her watch. The promotional tapings had gone longer than she'd anticipated, which meant that a few minutes were going to have to be edited out. Good, they could cut the part where she couldn't get the microwave door open.

The longer taping also meant she was late. She was supposed to have met Gil for lunch ten minutes earlier.

She got into her car, a four-year-old blue Toyota Tercel. Claire would never have been described as sentimental, especially by those who knew her best, but she loved that car. It was like an old friend who had seen her through many miles. Like her career, which had been up and down, down, down, up and down, down, and finally, at least for a while, up.

As she pulled out of her parking spot, she looked forward to seeing her husband, Gil.

DETECTIVE JASON HOLLIDAY frowned at the VCR. The red light was lit, the power still on.

"Has this been dusted?" he asked, pointing to it.

"Not yet," one of the techs said.

Holliday yanked a pair of rubber gloves from his pocket, the kind so thin that you could pick up a needle, and pulled them on with an audible snap. He took a pair of half glasses from his pocket, one of his few concessions to being fifty. He used them only at crime scenes or when he was typing a report.

He found the play button and pressed it, then stepped back to watch.

"What's this?" his partner asked.

He turned and looked at Detective Myra Longfellow. She was thirty-eight, had been a detective in St. Louis for only three years. All in all, she had thirteen years on the job. She and Holliday had been partners since she first received her gold shield, and he had taught her as much as he could. He wasn't happy back when they saddled him with the "rookie," but at the moment he was satisfied with their partnership. Hell, since his wife had moved in with her boy toy, Myra was the only woman whose company he even enjoyed.

Longfellow kept her iron gray hair layered and short,

favored pantsuits. She detested heels because they weren't practical in her line of work, but her love for shoes was satisfied by filling her closets with flats in every color, made of every fabric available.

"I know her," she said when the tape came on.

"Yeah? Who is she?"

"Her name is Claire Hunt," Longfellow said. "She's a host on the *Home Mall*."

"The what?" The only cable TV Holliday watched was ESPN.

"*Home Mall*—it's a shopping program," Longfellow said. "She must have been watching this when she was killed."

They both looked at the woman still propped up on the sofa. They had to wait for the medical examiner before they could move her.

"We don't know that she was killed," Holliday said.

Longfellow picked up the sofa cushion next to the corpse. "I'll bet this is the murder weapon."

"She was watching TV and just let somebody smother her with a pillow?"

"Ten bucks," Longfellow said.

"No bet." Holliday scowled. His partner's instincts were too good to bet against.

"So you think this is the same as the other one?" Holliday asked.

"I do. Not a mark on her."

Holliday frowned. "The other one was found propped up in bed, right?"

"Right."

"Smothered to death."

"Bed pillows make even better murder weapons."

Holliday stroked his jaw.

"If I remember correctly, there was a TV in the room."

"I think there was."

"And a VCR?"

Longfellow looked at her partner and said, "I guess we'd better check."

Holliday nodded. "And have the evidence boys bag the tape from this machine, just in case."

"You want to talk to Claire Hunt?" Longfellow asked.

Holliday shook his head. "Not yet. Let's wait and see what we get from the other apartment."

Longfellow nodded, started away to continue her examination of the apartment, then turned back.

"You know, one more and we got a serial."

Holliday made a face and waved the suggestion away. "Don't remind me."

TWO

GIL CHECKED HIS appearance in the bedroom mirror and, satisfied, walked into the living room. The apartment he shared with Claire was in a high-rise building on Brentwood Avenue in Clayton. He and Claire had moved there after they were first married. With the combined incomes from his store and her job as a hostess on the St. Louis-based *Home Mall* program, they were able to afford the rent. Prior to that, he'd lived in a more modest section of town in a small apartment he'd used primarily for sleeping. He'd moved there following his separation—and, ultimately, divorce—from his first wife, because it had been close enough for him to spend time with his two sons. Since that time, however, his wife had taken the boys and moved to New York. Now he got to see them only two or three times a year. It was actually a small price to pay not to have his ex living in the same town.

Gil had stopped home, leaving his bookstore in the hands of his sometime employee, Al Marcus. The Old Delmar Bookstore was housed in a trendy section of St. Louis named University City. The stretch of about six blocks along Delmar was known as the Loop. It boasted indoor and outdoor restaurants, antique shops, bookstores—two others besides his own—and small specialty shops catering to the college crowd.

Allyn Marcus was a good customer who always spent time in the store talking books with Gil, whether he bought something or not. Gil had taken to using him in the store whenever he wanted to get away—like today— to have lunch with his wife. Always wanting to look good for Claire, he had stopped home to freshen up.

Gil changed into his new leather jacket and left the apartment, heading for the Central West End, where they were meeting for lunch.

THE MOMENT Claire Hunt appeared, Gil's heart leapt a little. He'd never known a woman who had caused such a reaction in him. How lucky he felt that the excitement was still there after four years.

Gil Hunt was thirty-nine, three years younger than his wife, Claire, but his hair and beard were peppered with gray and this, coupled with her youthful looks, convinced people he was actually the older of the two.

Claire had an apologetic look on her face, which Gil found adorable.

"I'm sorry I'm late, Gil." She sat down opposite him and explained.

"Why don't you just go to Thurman?"

"I did. Well, I told Harve to tell Ben about the mike. I'm afraid I came off like a prima donna."

"You're entitled."

"Did you order?"

"I never order until you get here."

"You're sweet." She pushed away the menu that was in front of her. "I'm going to have the chili and a burger."

"I can hear your arteries hardening as we speak," he joked.

Culpeppers, in the West End, was one of Gil and

Claire's favorite spots, and they had a lot of them. St. Louis's West End was the city's version of New York's Greenwich Village. Three distinct sections and commercial areas were separated by blocks of private homes; the Pulitzers even had a small estate there. The intersections of the commercial areas were cobblestoned. Shade trees and huge ornate streetlamps looking more like chandeliers stuck on top of green poles lined the streets. Each area had its own restaurants and shops. In the spring and fall, the Hunts enjoyed sitting for hours, eating dinner, or just having coffee, while they people-watched.

Claire smiled across the table and Gil found, as he always did, inordinate pleasure in just looking at her. Her blond hair was shiny, and so clean that he could smell it. She had a straight nose that he found most attractive, and a wide mouth. She was intelligent, independent, loving, and easy to get along with—most of the time.

The waitress came over. Claire ordered her chili and burger.

"You want fries with that?"

"Sure."

"And you?"

"I'll have the Caesar salad," Gil said.

"Is that all?" She was young and attractive, and she smiled warmly at him. This was something Claire had trouble getting used to. Gil always seemed to be able to form a special bond with waitresses. He said it was because he treated them well; he even admitted to flirting with them.

He smiled and said, "I'll steal some of her fries."

When the waitress left, Claire asked, "Did she wink at you?"

Gil laughed, not quite sure if his wife was jealous or just pretending to be. She couldn't believe he was so naïve. His warm smile and gentleness weren't his only outstanding qualities. Those eyes of his, those big brown eyes, always made women want to approach him. How could he not know that by now? she wondered.

"So what do you want to do today?"

"I have to go back to the store," he said. "I've got a shipment coming in."

"When?"

"At four."

"And after that?"

"After that…nothing."

"Then I'll come by about four-thirty."

"Better make it six."

"Why?"

"Because that's when I close, Claire. You know that."

"Close early today."

"What do you have in mind?"

She winked. "I'll think of something." But she didn't have time to.

"Are you vibrating?" he asked, looking at her.

"Yes."

"I don't know why you wear that beeper."

She looked down at the gadget hooked on her belt and noticed the station's number flashing. "For the same reason everyone else wears one, love, so I can be annoyed at lunch. Excuse me."

She got up and walked to the pay phone by the door; she may have given in to Harve's request that she wear the infernal thing, but she would never be one of those people who carried a phone with her. She dialed the studio and asked for Harve Wilson, knowing he was the only one who would beep her.

"Claire?"

"What's so important, Harve, that it can't wait an hour?"

"Claire, the police are looking for you."

"What did you say?"

"You heard me. Cops."

"But why?"

"Mr. Thurman didn't say."

"What *did* he say, Harve?"

"He wants you to go to the Major Case Squad Office and talk to Detective Jason Holliday."

"About what?"

"I don't know, Claire," Wilson said, "but Mr. Thurman told them you'd be glad to cooperate any way you could."

"Sure, but I'd like to know what I'm cooperating about."

"Claire, do this today, as soon as possible."

"I'll do it right now," Claire said. "I want to find out what this is all about."

So did Gil. He decided to go to the police station with his wife.

"What about the store?" she asked, concerned.

"So I'll close early today."

THREE

THEY DROVE DOWNTOWN to the police station in separate cars. Inside, Gil asked at the front desk for Detective Holliday.

"Upstairs," the desk sergeant said. "First door on the right."

"Thanks."

"Ma'am?" the man asked, looking admiringly at Claire.

"I'm with him."

"Lucky him," the man said with a smile.

Gil gave the sergeant a cold look and took Claire's arm.

"He's just being nice," Claire said.

"I don't like idle flirting."

"Except with waitresses," she commented with an amused smile.

They went upstairs and into the squad room. There were several men sitting at desks, and one woman. The woman glanced at them, then looked away. One of the men, though, a bulky man in his fifties, acknowledged the couple, walked from his desk to the woman's, and said something to her. She looked up again as the male detective approached Claire and Gil. The woman got up after a beat and followed.

"Claire Hunt?"

"That's right."

"My name's Detective Jason Holliday. This is my partner, Detective Longfellow. We'd like to ask you a few questions."

"About what?" Gil asked.

"Who are you?"

"This is my husband, Gil," Claire said.

"It's about murder, Mr. Hunt."

"Murder?" Claire repeated.

"I'm afraid so, ma'am." The detective looked at Gil and said, "Maybe your husband could wait outside?"

"Why?" Claire asked. "I'll just have to tell him everything we talked about later. Letting him stay would save me the trouble."

"Well, all right," Holliday said. "Why don't you both come and sit at my desk?"

The four of them walked across the room to his desk.

"Detective Holliday, has someone I know been murdered?" Claire asked as he sat behind his desk and Longfellow stood next to him. Gil sat just behind Claire and to her left.

"That's what we'd like to know, Mrs. Hunt," Longfellow said. "Do you know a woman named Mary Dunn?"

"Mary Dunn…" Claire repeated, frowning, trying to place the name.

"Maybe a photo will help," Longfellow said.

"Uh, wait." Holliday stopped his partner before she could produce the photo. He looked at Claire. "The woman in the photo is dead, Mrs. Hunt."

"I appreciate the warning, Detective. Thank you. I think I can handle it."

Holliday nodded, and Longfellow took out the photo and placed it on the desk.

Claire picked it up and looked at it. "Jesus..." she said.

"I know," Holliday said. "She doesn't look dead. After she was murdered, she was propped up on the sofa. I think the killer made sure her eyes were open."

"Oh..." Claire said, and then looked uneasy, as if she hadn't realized she'd said it out loud. "How was she killed?"

"Suffocated," Longfellow said.

"It's a shock, I know, Mrs. Hunt," Holliday said.

"When was she murdered?" Gil asked.

"Last night, between ten and midnight."

Both detectives looked at Claire.

"You want to know where I was between those hours?"

"It would be nice," Longfellow said.

Claire shrugged. "Home."

"By yourself?"

"No," Gil said. "With me. Is Claire a suspect?"

Holliday smiled at Claire, and Gil almost expected him to pat her hand.

"Not at all, Mr. Hunt, Mrs. Hunt. It's just routine right now."

"Please don't patronize me, Detective," Claire said.

Holliday looked alarmed.

"I wasn't, Mrs. Hunt. There's no reason to suspect you of anything...at the moment."

"Then why am I here?" Claire asked.

"Mrs. Hunt, did you know a woman named Kathleen Sands?" Longfellow asked.

"Sands?" Claire repeated. "I don't think—"

"I thought this was about a woman named Mary Dunn," Gil said.

"Mr. Hunt," Holliday said, "please don't interfere."

"What? Hey—"

Claire turned and put her hand on his arm. "Gil, please." She looked at Longfellow then and said, "Kathleen Sands?"

"That's right."

"The name doesn't ring a bell."

"How about this?" Longfellow handed over a picture.

Obviously, the girl was dead also, posed similarly to the other, except she was on a bed. She had long dark hair and in life had probably been stunning.

"No," she said, returning the photo.

Longfellow took it and exchanged a glance with her partner.

"All right, Mrs. Hunt, thank you for coming in."

"That's it?"

Holliday smiled and said, "For now."

"Is it against the rules for you to tell me why you called me in? Why did you think I knew these women?"

"That's not really something—" Longfellow began, but Holliday—exercising his right as senior partner, no doubt—interrupted her.

"At the time they were murdered, both women were watching videotapes of your television show, Mrs. Hunt," Holliday said. "That's how you became involved."

"They both watched my show?" Claire asked, surprised.

"We don't know if they were regular viewers, Mrs. Hunt," Holliday said, "but when they were found, each of the VCRs had a tape of your show in it."

"I don't understand," Gil said.

"Frankly, Mr. Hunt," Holliday said, "neither do we. When we do, however, maybe we can explain it to you. Once again, thanks for coming in."

Claire felt as if she should ask more questions, but she couldn't think of any.

"Claire…" Gil said, putting his hand on her shoulder.

"Right." She stood up.

As they left, Holliday and Longfellow looked after them thoughtfully.

"What do you think?" Longfellow asked.

"I'm not sure," Holliday said. "She seems to be honestly puzzled."

"I think she's dirty."

"Why?"

"I don't know," she said, "just a feeling."

"You always think attractive women are dirty."

"Are you accusing me of being catty, or just bitchy?"

"Catty," he said, "definitely catty."

FOUR

WHEN THEY WERE outside the police station, Claire asked Gil, "So what are you thinking?"

"I'm thinking that you knew the first woman they asked about."

"Maybe. Was it that obvious?"

"Only to me. Where'd you know her from?"

"That's just it—I can't remember."

They walked down the steps and started toward the municipal parking lot.

"What are we going to do now?" she asked.

"About what?"

His lack of interest irritated her. "About the murders. Aren't you curious? Even a little?"

"Sure, but I don't know what you expect me to do."

She stopped short next to a newspaper machine and bought a copy of the *St. Louis Post-Dispatch*. The front page carried side-by-side photos of two women. "Both victims were found with a cassette tape of my show in their VCRs. That's some coincidence."

"What else could it be, Claire?"

"I don't know, but I'd sure like to find out."

Gil frowned. "Don't tell me you want to drag us into a police investigation."

"We've already been drug in, my dear husband," she

said as they reached their cars. "I would think you'd want to do your best to keep me out of jail."

Gil hesitated a moment, then said, "Well, I guess I *would* miss you if they put you in the big house."

"So what should we do first?"

"I guess we could start by seeing Mr. Thurman. Apparently, the police went to him to get to you."

"That's a great idea. I knew you'd think of something."

When they reached their cars, which were parked next to each other, he asked, "Where to?"

"To talk to Ben. Isn't that what you just said we should do?"

"Well, I didn't mean right now."

"Now's as good a time as any." She opened her car door. "I'll meet you there."

BENJAMIN THURMAN HAD an office in the TBN building on Grand Boulevard, but he didn't keep regular hours there. He had other businesses and holdings and another office in the Famous Barr building in downtown St. Louis.

Claire pulled into her reserved parking spot and waited for Gil to park in a visitor's space. They walked into the studio together.

At the moment, a local news program, also directed by Harve Wilson, was airing. The anchors were a man who formerly had been with a national network but who had been let go because of his age, and an attractive young blonde who Thurman was hoping would blossom into a top anchorwoman. There was no way Claire could get to Harve at that moment. She looked around and spotted Linda Bennett, who was sitting on a stool eating an apple and watching the proceedings. Linda always hung around in case there was need for an extra cameraperson. She collected overtime the way some people collected stamps.

Linda Bennett was in her late twenties, a woman with arresting good looks, due to her turquoise eyes and full lips. Her hair was long and straight, a mixture of reds and browns, and although she was slender, Claire knew she worked out and kept herself toned.

"Linda." Claire came up next to her and spoke in a low voice. Gil stayed one step behind.

Linda turned her head and smiled when she saw Claire. The smile broadened when she saw Gil.

"Hi, Claire…" she said, and then, in a completely different tone, added, "Hello, Gil."

"Hi, Linda."

"What are you doin' back here?" she asked Claire.

"I'm looking for Mr. Thurman. Have you seen him?"

"I think he's upstairs. He was down here chewing Harve out about half an hour ago."

"What for?"

"I couldn't hear," she said, shaking her head. She had a bandanna around her neck. She often used one to hold her hair back when she was working. "But I didn't see him leave."

"Thanks."

"Trouble?"

"I'm not sure." Claire put her hand on Linda's arm. "I'll talk to you later."

Linda smiled past Claire at Gil. "See you, Gil."

"Bye, Linda."

At the back of the studio, they went through a door leading to a stairway, took that to the second floor, then walked along the hall until coming to a door marked JANITOR. Ben Thurman liked to believe he had an off-beat sense of humor. When he converted the warehouse into a television studio, with offices on the second floor, instead of having his name stenciled across the door, he left the original large black letters. Claire's theory was that it would make people think he was humble—but Benjamin Thurman was quite the opposite.

Claire knocked and they entered. There was an outer office for a secretary, but Thurman didn't have one— not at this location anyway. The door to the inner office was open and they could hear Thurman talking. Claire checked the phone on the desk and saw one of the lines was lit. They waited until they heard Thurman hang up and then made their presence known.

"Anybody around?"

"In here. Is that you, Claire?"

"It's me, Ben."

"Come on in."

Claire entered the office and saw Thurman standing behind his desk. Her boss was in his fifties, healthy, robust, still had a full head of brown hair. Claire suspected Thurman wore his hair slicked back and wet because it appeared darker and hid traces of gray.

He was wearing one of the western shirts he'd ordered from a catalog. This one was black on one side, with a mass of multicolored shapes, mostly reds, yellows, and oranges, scattered on the other. Thurman liked to wear western clothes, right down to the boots; it was the only thing he willingly spent money on. The man had been born in Texas, but his family had moved to St. Louis when he was two years old. Nevertheless, there were times when he affected a Texas twang, and this was one of them.

"Oh, hello, Gil. I should have guessed.... Tell me

what the hell happened with the cops.'' He motioned Claire to sit down.

"I thought you would have known all about it," Claire said.

"Hell, all I know is that they were lookin' for you. Fill me in on all the details.''

Claire gave Thurman a straightforward report. Gil decided to stand back for a while, just to watch and listen. He knew that somewhere in that egotistical heart, Ben Thurman had a soft spot for Claire.

When she had finished, Thurman rubbed his chin. "Holliday, that's the one I talked to.''

"What did he say?''

"He asked for you, said he would appreciate it if you would come in and talk to him.''

"And you didn't ask what it was about?''

"I sure did. He told me it was just a routine inquiry. I didn't think cops really said that.''

"Well, I guess they do," Claire said. "Those were his exact words to us.''

"Do they suspect you, Claire?''

"They said no, but isn't it their job to suspect everyone?''

"You didn't even know the women, did you?''

"No," Claire said, and left it at that. Gil silently agreed with her decision.

"What now, Ben?''

He looked confused. "What do you mean?''

"Are you thinking about pulling me off the air?''

"Why on earth would I do that?''

"Come on, I know how conservative you can be.''

"Maybe, but why would you expect me to overreact like that? There's no scandal here, right, Claire?''

"None that I know of.''

"Then don't worry."

"What about the tapes, Ben?" Gil asked.

"What about them?"

"Have there been any videos of Claire's show distributed?"

"A little old home-shopping program? Come on, Gil, this is not *Bonanza* we're doing here, you know? No, there are no tapes."

"So the ones the cops found had to be homemade." Gil was almost speaking to himself.

"That's good news, isn't it?" Thurman asked, looking at Claire. "There are women out there who are taping your show. Maybe we're a bigger hit than we think, huh?"

"Yeah," Claire said, "and they're dying to see it, right?"

FIVE

THE NEXT DAY WAS Saturday. Gil didn't usually open the store until one, and Claire was not scheduled to work. Claire woke first, and Gil remained in bed until the fragrant hints of breakfast filled the air. He followed the aroma of coffee and bacon into the kitchen, wearing only a pair of Jockey shorts. She was wearing a green floral-print robe that came midthigh.

As he entered the room, he took her into his arms and kissed her.

"Careful, sweetie." Claire held a spatula coated with scrambled eggs.

"Good morning to you, too." He sat himself at the table.

She carried a cup of coffee to him. "So what do you think?"

"Since when are you so chatty in the morning?"

She smoothed down his ruffled hair. "I've been thinking about it all night. It's driving me crazy. I can't remember where I knew that poor woman from."

"The one in the first picture the police showed you?"

"Yes, Mary Dunn. Do you think if the police find out that I did know her, they'll think I lied on purpose? To protect myself because I'm involved with all this somehow? What do you think?"

In spite of how anxious his wife was, Gil told her

what he honestly thought, no matter how much it might upset her. "If you said you knew her but couldn't remember where you'd met, I guess that would sound fishy. So maybe, in a weird way, you did lie. I better call Anson; you should have a lawyer."

She sat down across the table from him and buttered the toast. "I haven't done anything. Besides, Anson's not a criminal lawyer."

"Lots of people who haven't done anything go to jail, Claire." Gil slowly chewed on a piece of bacon. "Maybe Anson can recommend someone."

"I'm not a suspect, Gil. The police said so."

"Even the police lie. I still think you should talk to a lawyer...."

Over their last cup of coffee, he told her, "I'm supposed to go to a book fair at two."

"You'd better hustle, then."

"I don't have to go."

"Yes you do; it's your business." She smiled at her doting husband. "I'm fine."

He kissed her neck and left the kitchen. He went directly to the bathroom to shower. *Lament for a Dead Cowboy* by Catherine Dain was laying on Claire's vanity. She was hopelessly hooked on female private-eye fiction, and Gil found it odd for someone as sophisticated as his wife was supposed to be. Then again, he was the one who had gotten her the copy of Sue Grafton's *"L" Is for Lawless* that was on her nightstand.

IT WAS 12:45 by the time he was ready to leave. She was sitting in the living room, reading *Snapshot* by Linda Barnes.

"I don't know anyone else who has a book for each room," he said.

She smiled and put the book down. "I can't help it. I don't want to waste time having to look for the same book all the time."

She walked him to the door.

"Will you please think about a lawyer?" he asked.

"I'll think about it."

He turned to face her at the door and took hold of her elbows. He started to say one thing, then stopped and said something else. "That's all I ask."

She hugged him tightly, then kissed him.

"I'll be at the store until six, and then we can go to dinner."

"Sure."

He kissed her again and left.

On the way down in the elevator, he thought about how people always panicked when the police came into their lives. He guessed it was much the same reaction they had toward the IRS.

As he exited the elevator and walked through the lobby, he wondered if they needed a criminal lawyer. And if so, how would he go about getting one?

SIX

THE WEEKEND HAD relaxed them. Flower boxes on the balcony were crowded with dozens of daffodils and the mid-April days were warm enough to sit outside. Unconsciously, they had insulated themselves—no television, no newspapers, no complications. And it had worked...at least for two days. When Monday eventually dawned, Gil and Claire were forced out into the rain to begin a new week.

GETTING UP AT 4:00 a.m. and making it to the studio by 5:30 was the pits. But the morning show was Claire's baby. She had worked hard to secure the 7:00 a.m. spot for five consecutive programming days each week. Once she arrived at the studio, she went directly to her small cubicle behind the set, next to the dressing rooms, and reviewed the product lineup for her shows. After finishing her third cup of tea, she combed her hair and did her own makeup, with barely enough time left to gulp down her orange juice. Then she headed for the set.

The *Home Mall* theme song started up and while a promo for an upcoming program was being aired, Harve shouted to her. An assistant grabbed the paper cup from Claire's hand, another adjusted her microphone. For a second, there wasn't a sound, everyone froze in place. Then the prerecorded tape concluded, the large hour hand of the station's clock touched the very top, and it was showtime.

"Good morning, St. Louis, it's a dreary day, but that makes it all the more fun to stay home and shop. I'm Claire Hunt and I'll be your host for the next four hours. This morning, we'll be talking about western jewelry." She smiled into the camera.

Dressed in a denim shirt, seated behind a waist-high table, Claire held up a turquoise ring. Each segment of her program had been researched and was meant to entertain as well as to sell products.

"I bet you didn't know that turquoise is called 'the guardian gem.' The American Indians used to put pieces of the stone in the beams of their homes for good luck. The blue of the turquoise was believed to represent the sky. Medicine men used turquoise in healing ceremonies; this particular ring was made by the Navajo. We have it in sizes five through nine."

A small clock was displayed in the lower right-hand corner of the viewer's screen. Ticking down two minutes, it urged customers to call in before supplies ran out.

Hosts on the *Home Mall* show not only had to be friendly but also able to ad lib, relate personal anecdotes that tied in with featured items. It had always come easily to Claire, who was well traveled, well read, and well liked.

"Now remember, when cleaning your turquoise jewelry, don't use any harsh detergents or commercial products. The vivid blue of the stone can change color. Just polish it with a soft cloth.

"I remember a little charm I received from my grandmother when I was about ten years old." The memory of her eccentric grandma always made Claire happy.

"Whenever she traveled, she never forgot to bring me a souvenir for my charm bracelet. I thought I was being so careful and dipped it in some of my mother's silver polish. I still have the bracelet, but that particular charm turned a funny shade of blue."

Harve's voice spoke to her from the small earpiece hidden by her hair. "There's a woman calling from Chicago; her name is Helen."

Without missing a beat, Claire slipped the ring on her finger and said, "Hi, Helen, how's the weather in Chicago today?"

"Pretty wet, Claire."

"Guess that's to be expected this time of year. So tell me, what do you like about this ring?"

The caller went on with her comments and Claire monitored the seconds clicking away. Knowing how very precious airtime was, Claire thanked Helen from Chicago for calling and was about to say good-bye, but the caller wasn't quite ready to hang up.

"Claire, you're my very favorite host."

"Well, I thank you for that. It's always nice to—"

"I don't know if you remember me or not, but we met when you were at the Fox Theater with your family. My husband and I drove down to St. Louis on business and decided to see *Cats*. I was the lady with the big corsage. It was Mother's Day. Remember?"

"Of course I do. You were wearing a lilac suit."

"That's right!"

Even though Claire had been an on-air celebrity for more than three years, it still surprised her how thrilled people were to just speak to her or meet her on the street. It was all baffling in a wonderful way.

"Well, Helen, I don't mean to rush you, but we do have to move on."

"Oh, that's all right. You take care, and, honey, don't worry about those awful stories in the paper; we're all behind you."

She didn't show her surprise over that last comment; after all, Claire was a professional. "Thanks, Helen, and I hope you enjoy your ring. Remember everything here at the *Home Mall* comes with a thirty-day money-back guarantee."

Claire knew there was no way she could find out what had appeared in the papers until her time slot wrapped up. Quickly, she reassured herself that while Chicago reporters might find the story of a murder in a neighboring city newsworthy, other cities had much more important items to concern themselves with. Besides, it was so early in the morning that her viewers were busy eating breakfast and getting ready for work; they probably hadn't even picked up on what Helen was referring to.

"Our next item is a beautiful black onyx and sterling silver pair of earrings. Onyx is believed to increase concentration and devotion. It's supposed to get rid of nightmares and ease tension." I should cover myself in this stuff, Claire thought, but she said, "I love the jet black richness of these earrings. The stones are round-cut and centered between two silver petals."

Time seemed to move along fast enough; Claire loved her job and jewelry was one of her passions. She often thought she would have loved to be a designer, but that occupation would have to wait for another lifetime.

There were bracelets and more rings, pendants and pins. Before the hour came to an end, another call was taken.

"Hi, you're on the air with Claire. Who's this, please?"

"Loretta from Denver."

"Ah, the Mile High City. You live in a beautiful part of the country, Loretta."

"I sure do."

Sometimes the callers had to be coaxed, and sometimes it was hard to get them to stop talking.

"Don't you just love western jewelry?" Claire asked.

"Yes, I do. It's beautiful."

"And which item did you purchase today?" Claire watched the hands of the studio clock, swearing they had stopped.

"The man's ring for my husband. The one with the eagle."

"What a nice choice, Loretta; I hope he enjoys it."

Suddenly, the woman became talkative, evidently more interested in gossiping than shopping. "I heard what that last caller said, and, Claire, I just wanted to tell you we're all out here for you. You're one great lady and we love you."

Please, don't say any more, Claire silently begged, but the woman was too quick. "We all know you could never hurt anyone. Why, you're like a member of our own family."

Claire's smile never wavered, not one bit. "Thank you, Loretta. Tell your husband we say hi."

"Well," she said into the camera, "that about wraps it up for our western-jewelry hour. Please stay tuned while Beth Anne tells you what's coming up later today. I'll be right back with today's deal of the day—the lowest price we've ever had on our luxurious one hundred percent silk jackets."

As soon as the tape started rolling, Claire dashed for her dressing room to change into the deal of the day. While she was fretting over which color would look best, Harve came charging toward her.

"Claire, Ben says he wants to see you."

"I thought so," Claire said. "Tell him I'll be up around eleven."

"He says now, Claire."

"But I'm on in a minute, Harve; you know that."

"Beth is doing a special presentation of the deal—it should take fifteen minutes—so get upstairs, now."

"All right already." Claire started to hang up the jacket in her hand, so as not to wrinkle the fabric.

"Run, Claire. Hurry!" Harve seemed crazed.

"Okay, okay!"

SEVEN

GIL USED TO FEEL guilty about being able to stay in bed for hours after Claire headed down to the station. But as time went by, he reasoned that his wife loved her job almost as much as she loved him. And keeping that job meant turning in early as well as getting up early. It really didn't have much to do with him at all. Besides, he loved his books—almost as much as her—and the quiet time, late at night, when he could just sit and read. Friends used to tell them that their arrangement wouldn't work out, that the couple that went to bed together stayed together. But their relationship had defied most all of the other rules, so why not that one, as well?

After stretching out onto Claire's side of the bed, Gil slowly opened his eyes, remembering it was Monday. Getting up, he took a quick shower then headed for the kitchen. On his way through the living room, he turned on the television set to check in on his wife. It had gotten past the point of being strange, the idea that he could see how Claire looked and what she was doing just by turning on the television set.

He noticed she was holding up some kind of ring—all jewelry looked the same to him—and she was wearing what appeared to be a cowboy shirt. He smiled, thinking she looked good in anything she wore.

Gil was finishing up his breakfast when the phone

rang. He hated talking with anyone before noon. Even though his business dictated that he socialize the minute he opened his store, that didn't mean he had to be polite while still in his bathrobe. He started to let the answering machine take the call until he recognized his mother's voice.

"Gil? I see you sitting there! Come on, darling, be a good boy and pick up."

He couldn't help himself, and he walked to the phone. "Are you sure you got the right number, lady?"

"It's nice to hear you so happy…considering."

"Considering what?"

"Enough with the jokes, Gil; I called to find out how you and Claire are holding up. I tried to hold off until you called me, but I just couldn't wait any longer. So? Tell me," Rose Hunterelli implored her son. Hunterelli was Gil's family name. When he first opened his bookstore, he realized that with his mail-order business, he'd be on the phone a lot, explaining not only how to pronounce his name but how to spell it. Shortening it to Hunt for business purposes seemed the thing to do.

"I don't know what you're talking about, Ma. No kidding."

"Honey…" Rose began slowly, not quite sure how to ask her question, or if she even should. "Do you have the television on?"

"Yes, I'm watching Claire's show."

"Well, maybe you should turn to a real channel. Try ABC; they're having the local news in a minute or so."

"But, Ma—"

"Go do it, Gil. I'll hang on."

He didn't want to tell here—again—that the kitchen phone was a cordless model and he could talk to her while he walked. Instead, he silently picked up the remote control and pushed number 1 first and then the 2. Walking back to the dining room table, he positioned himself in such a way so that he had a good view of the screen.

"Now what? What am I watching for?"

"Be patient," his mother said. "Ever since you were a little boy, you never liked to wait for anything...."

While Rose chattered into the receiver, Gil watched the television. Finally, a familiar anchorwoman in a red jacket came into focus. Gil expected the story to feature the two murdered women the police had questioned Claire about. He knew sooner or later it would all get into the news. But he was caught completely off guard when the panic started pulsing in his temples as the television screen was filled with Claire's latest publicity photo.

"I'll call you back, Ma; I want to hear this."

The anchorwoman was already into her story when Gil turned up the volume.

"Sources have informed us that Claire Hunt, host on the popular *Home Mall*, has been implicated in the murders of two women found slain in their homes. Videotapes of Hunt's shopping program were found at both scenes, leading police to target her for investigation. We'll have more on this story as the facts come in. Just to recap, a St. Louis television personality has been brought in for questioning in the murders of two women." As she continued, the reporter looked up into the camera and smiled, confiding to her audience. "Scandal has been known to advance many careers. Could Claire Hunt be headed for fame or infamy? Watch tonight after our regular ten o'clock broadcast for a special report on 'Scandal: Stepping-Stone or Headstone.'

"In other news—"

Gil switched back to TBN. A different hostess was talking about a jacket. Gil dialed the station and asked for Claire.

"I'm sorry, Mr. Hunt, your wife is in a meeting right now."

"But she's supposed to be on the air." Gil couldn't understand the change in schedule. "Okay, then, let me talk to Harve Wilson, please."

"Just one moment."

"Gil"—Harve sounded out of breath—"this is not a good time. I'll have Claire call you as soon as she gets out of Thurman's office."

"A minute, Harve. Come on, I need to know what's happening."

"If I knew something, I'd tell you, Gil. Honest. You're just going to have to find out when the rest of us do."

"It's just that—"

"I know, Gil, and I'm real sorry."

"Thanks anyway."

"No problem."

After looking at the receiver for a moment, Gil reluctantly hung up. The only thing he could do now was open the store and wait.

"WHAT DO YOU MEAN, 'keep it up'? Do you think I enjoy being put in a situation like this?" Claire sat down, trying not to raise her voice.

"Ya'll didn't kill anyone, did you, Claire?"

"What? How on earth can you ask me—"

"Then I don't see why you're getting so upset." Benjamin Thurman leaned against the wall, balancing on two legs of his large wooden chair.

She massaged the side of her neck. "I am getting

upset because I'm the one out there trying to smile while our customers—"

"Correction, Claire, your *fans*. They aren't just customers—that's the whole point. That sweet lady from Chicago, she loves you. Didn't she say so?"

"It was the woman from Denver who said she loved me. And, Ben, I don't see how that has anything to do with murder."

"Denver, Chicago, Fort Wayne, or Houston—there are people out there who care about you. The other day, when you asked me if I was planning on pulling you off the air, I wasn't sure what I was going to do. It's not like this sort of thing happens every day. But now, hearing the concern out there, I know how important it is that you go on every day. That you show your public you're dealing with everything just fine. After all, Claire, honesty is what we here at TBN are all about."

"And I just thought it was all about sales and percentiles."

Thurman let his chair drop back onto the floor. "I'm not gonna lie about that. We're running a business here. But we're selling the truth as well as our products. There isn't one item out there that I wouldn't stake my reputation on. How can you expect anyone to trust you if you don't give them the truth? Why, people can read a lie in your eyes."

For a moment, Claire felt guilty. It was Benjamin Thurman's integrity that had convinced her to take the job hosting the *Home Mall* show in the first place. "I suppose you're right about me facing all of it."

"That's a girl. Now go back down there and show 'em what you're made of. I was thinking that maybe we should increase our calls from three an hour to five or six."

GIL WALKED TO the back of the store, savoring the sound of creaking floorboards and the scent of paper and leather bindings. He never got tired of the way the store smelled. But even being surrounded by his beloved books could not comfort him this morning; all he could think about was his wife. When the phone rang, he jumped for it, startled.

"Old Delmar Bookstore."

"Gil? It's Paul. How are you guys doing? Is my mom okay?"

Paul Duncan lived in Kansas City. After graduating with a degree in criminal justice, he had decided any job requiring a tie or suit was not for him. One interview with social services, and he got himself hired as head guide for the Gangster Tour, happily spending his days pointing out old bullet holes left by Prohibition tommy guns. Paul was a six-foot-tall twenty-three-year-old—as far as earth years were concerned. Physically, he looked more like he was eighteen, and spiritually, he was Yoda.

"She's fine, Paul; not to worry. The police questioned her a few days ago; that's all that's happened so far."

"I was driving to work this morning and when I turned on the radio, there she was, all over the news. Gosh, my dad would never be involved in anything this cool."

Claire's first husband, Frank, had remarried and was living in Anaheim, right next door to Mickey Mouse. Theirs had been such an easy divorce. But then, their marriage had been so calm, so uneventful that now, years later, Claire had a difficult time remembering much about it.

"I'm waiting to call her when she gets off the air."

"Well, I was kinda worried."

Gil had liked the kid from the very beginning. "We're

fine. Why don't you call your mother tonight after things calm down a bit.''

"Okay. And, pseudo-Dad, take care of yourself, too.''

"I always do.'' Gil was unexpectedly touched by Paul's concern and found it difficult to keep his voice even.

"Do not,'' Paul joked.

"Do too.''

EIGHT

OVER THE COURSE of the next ten days, Gil and Claire did not hear a word from the police. They were relieved enough even to stop thinking about a lawyer. There was nothing more in the newspaper about the two women who had been murdered. Everything seemed right with the world.

Except for a woman named Susie Kennedy.

SUSIE WAS EXCITED. In all her thirty-two years, she had never won anything. Her life—except for the few years back in her early twenties, when she used to follow the Cardinals down to Florida for spring training—had been dull, dull, dull. Now suddenly, she'd won a contest and had a chance to appear on the *Home Mall* show with Claire Hunt.

The call had come out of the blue, a complete surprise. She argued that she hadn't entered anything, but the man on the phone told her it was a random drawing. You didn't even have to be a fan of the program. She wasn't, but it was still exciting to think about appearing on television. He also said she would get two hundred "*Home Mall* dollars." She couldn't turn that down.

She looked at her watch, then checked her hair again in the bathroom mirror. A representative was coming over to see if she presented a "telegenic appearance."

She loved that phrase. She could tell her friends and family for the rest of her life that she had once been "telegenic."

It was 7:00 p.m., the time the man was supposed to arrive. She smoothed her green skirt over her thighs, ruffled the front of her lavender silk blouse, and turned her head to check her amethyst earrings. She'd agonized over what hose to wear, then decided she couldn't go wrong with black.

At 7:10, her doorbell rang. She caught herself rushing to answer it, then slowed down. When she reached the door, she took a deep breath before opening it.

There stood an odd-looking man in the hall. He had a mass of curly hair and the bushiest mustache she had ever seen. He was tall, trim, but not exactly the kind of guy she'd ever think of going out with.

"Are you from TBN?" she asked.

"That's right."

She put on her hundred-watt smile. "Please, come in...."

"WE JUST WANT YOU to watch a particular segment of the show and give us some feedback," the killer said.

"You mean I get to pick my own segment?" she asked as the man popped a tape into her VCR.

"Oh, yes, we want you to be as comfortable as possible, Miss Kennedy."

"But...am I telegenic enough?" she asked hopefully.

The killer hadn't even known if that was a real word when he'd first contacted her. He turned and looked at her, sitting there on the sofa, knees clenched together, all dressed in green and purple, and fought to keep from laughing.

"Oh, yes, you're just what we're looking for."

He pressed the play button on the VCR, then walked around to stand behind her.

"Just watch...."

There was some static, and then Claire Hunt appeared on the screen.

"Today is fashion day and we're going to show you some fantastic items to help spruce up your wardrobe." As Claire spoke, Susie visualized herself standing next to the hostess, on television, with thousands, maybe millions of people watching.

"Is this the part—" she began, but the man shushed her.

"Just watch, please."

He looked to his right and then his left. There were velvet pillows scattered the length of the sofa. All of them were purple. Must be her favorite color, he thought, picking one up. He held it a moment, just behind her head, and then repeated, "Just watch...."

NINE

"Two weeks," Myra Longfellow said, "two weeks to the day. Coincidence?"

"Probably," Holliday said, looking around. "It wasn't two weeks between victims one and two, though, so it doesn't appear to be a pattern."

There was a lot of activity in the apartment: detectives, technicians, photographers, all moving about, doing their jobs. It was Holliday's job to catch this bastard, so it looked like he was the only one who wasn't getting it done.

"What do you want to do about the tapes?" Longfellow asked.

Holliday sighed. "Let's call Claire Hunt in again. We know she's not a coincidence."

"I think she's dirty, Jace. I told you that two weeks ago."

"I know you did. But I didn't understand it then and I still don't. How come you've never even considered the idea that she might be the next victim? I know I have."

"Don't be silly." Longfellow laughed at the thought. "We should have put surveillance on her."

"We didn't have enough probable cause, or manpower," he reminded her.

"How about now?"

''Probable cause, maybe,'' he said, ''but we still don't have the manpower.''

Holliday looked down at the dead woman, who still seemed to be watching the television. The bastard. Even if she had died with her eyes closed, he was willing to bet the killer had opened them again. All of it was his trademark. This guy was trying to slice himself a piece of history. Son of Sam, Ted Bundy, the Hillside Strangler—what were the newspapers going to call this one?

''What are you thinking?'' Longfellow asked.

Holliday rubbed his hands over his face before answering. ''I was wondering when I had my last vacation.''

''Last year, same as me.''

He looked at her. ''I'm wondering why I bothered coming back.''

''Huh?''

He shook his head. ''Never mind.''

He got one of the photographers who was taking pictures with a Polaroid to take an extra one of the woman. He wanted to keep it with the others.

''What are you gonna do with that?'' his partner asked. ''You collecting them?''

He ignored her question. ''Come on, let's go and see Claire Hunt ourselves.''

''Now you're talkin'.''

TEN

HOLLIDAY AND LONGFELLOW didn't find Claire Hunt at home, and she wasn't at work. They talked to a couple of technicians at the studio, but they didn't know anything regarding her whereabouts. Thurman wasn't in his office at the moment, so there was no one else at TBN for them to talk to.

That was the reason they walked into Gil's bookstore at three o'clock that afternoon and found him sitting at his desk, talking on the phone.

When Gil spotted the two detectives, he motioned to them, asking for a moment of patience.

"That's right, Mrs. Daly," he said into the phone, "I would do an evaluation on the spot. No, I wouldn't make you wait like some of the others are doing. Yes, Saturday would be fine. No, I'm afraid I'm not up that early. How about one o'clock? Fine, I'll see you then."

Hanging up the phone, he looked at Detectives Holliday and Longfellow.

"The lady's husband died, leaving behind a large book collection. I'm just one of several dealers hoping to examine it, and possibly bid. She, uh, wanted me to stop by her house at eight a.m. on Saturday."

"I don't understand why older people get up so early," Holliday said. "It's not as if they have someplace important to go. I got an aunt started getting up at five a.m. soon as she hit sixty. Me, when I hit fifty, I started getting up earlier, though not that—''

Longfellow cut her partner off by clearing her throat.

"Right," Holliday said. "Mr. Hunt, we're looking for your wife. She's not at home, and she's not at her studio. Do you know where she might be?''

"I'd be a poor excuse for a husband if I didn't.''

"Lots of husbands think they know where their wives are, Mr. Hunt," Longfellow said. "But it's been our experience that this isn't always the case.''

"I know where Claire is, Detective Longfellow.''

"Well, that's good," she said. "Would you might enlightening us?''

Gil found it easy to dislike the woman, so he turned his attention to her partner.

"What's this about?''

"We just have some more questions for her," Holliday said.

"Concerning what?''

"Mr. Hunt—'' Longfellow began, but this time it was Holliday who interrupted her.

"Myra," he said, and she backed off with a scowl. "Mr. Hunt, we found another murdered woman.''

"Oh no.'' Gil said, sincerely disturbed by the news.

"Yes," Holliday said, "and there's another tape in the VCR at the scene.''

"Jesus…''

"Is your wife in town, sir?" Holliday asked.

"No, she's not," Gil said. "She's on a…well, a sort of buying trip. Sometimes the station sends their hosts into the field to look at items; Claire's in Chicago today.''

"When did she leave?" Longfellow asked.

"Early this morning.''

"Did she fly?" Holliday asked.

"She prefers to drive. She enjoys road trips."

Longfellow looked at Holliday. "Enough time," she said.

Gil shoved his chair across the wooden floor and bolted to his feet. "Now wait a minute—"

"Don't get upset, Mr. Hunt." Holliday held his hand out like a traffic cop. "That's not gonna do anybody any good."

"But you can't possibly think—"

"We're just here to ask a few questions, Mr. Hunt," Holliday said reasonably. "If you answer them, this will go real smooth."

Gil, naturally protective of the woman he loved, realized he had to back off a bit before he ended up incriminating her somehow.

"Okay," he said, "ask your questions."

"The dead woman was Susan Kennedy. Does that name ring a bell?"

"No. I don't know any Susan Kennedy."

"Her neighbors tell us she was called Susie."

"Sorry," Gil said with a shrug.

"What about your wife?" Longfellow asked. "Would she have known a Susie Kennedy?"

"She might."

"When will she be home, Mr. Hunt?" she asked.

"In three days—on Sunday."

"And you didn't go with her because you have to look at this book collection on Saturday?"

"That's right."

"So, she's in Chicago, all alone until Sunday, huh?" Longfellow asked.

"Yes, detective, she is."

"Guess you must trust her a lot, huh?"

"I love her," Gil said, "and yes, I trust her—we trust each other."

"Hmm," Longfellow said, looking around the store.

"Don't mind my partner, Mr. Hunt," Holliday said. "She's a little on the cynical side. Comes with the job, I guess."

"And you're not cynical, Detective Holliday?" Gil asked.

"Oh, sure I am." Holliday shifted his weight uncomfortably. "I just don't let it show as much. Do you still have my card, Mr. Hunt?"

"I have it."

"Good. Would you have your wife get back to me when she returns? We'd like to set up a time to talk to her about Susan Kennedy."

"I can ask her about it tonight, when she calls me."

"From Chicago," Myra Longfellow said.

"That's right," Gil replied sharply, "from Chicago." Turning toward the woman, he asked, "Has it ever—even once—occurred to you that Claire could be the one in danger here?"

"Hmm," Longfellow said, and walked out.

"Yes, it's crossed our minds, Mr. Hunt," Holliday said, "that's why we want to keep an eye on her." He followed his partner.

Gil watched them through his front window as they got into their car, Holliday doing the driving. He scolded himself for letting the female detective get to him with her snide remarks.

THAT NIGHT, when he spoke with Claire on the phone, she sensed he was upset.

"She's only trying to get under your skin, sweetie."

"I know."

"You can't let her do that."

"I know, I know. I just don't like anybody thinking bad things about you."

"I love you," she said.

"I love you more."

"No, you don't."

"Okay."

"Pig."

"Claire? Are you sure the name doesn't sound familiar at all?"

"Susan—Susie Kennedy?" Claire repeated the name. "No, it doesn't. Did they show you a photo?"

"No," he said. "They'll probably save that pleasure for you."

"I'll look forward to it. What's going on, Gil? Is someone trying to...to hang something on me by leaving these tapes at the murder scenes?"

"I don't know, hon. I don't know what to think, but when you get back, maybe we better do something about finding out."

"You mean investigate?" She sounded excited.

"I mean ask some questions and see if we can't find out what's going on."

"I think that's called investigating, Gil."

"You call it what you want," he said. "I just call it keeping the woman I love out of jail."

"Would you wait for me? If they put me in jail?"

"Well, I guess I could. Would I have to go visit you?"

"You're damn right you would," she said. "I'd want my conjugal rights."

"Okay, then."

The banter was forced, and they both knew it.

"Gil, we'll figure this out."

"Sure we will, honey."

"Should I come home early?"

"No," he said. "Let's not let them change our routine. You do your job, visit MaryJane—the two of you always have a great time together—and then come home."

"Maybe you could nose around while I'm gone."

"You know," he said, "I was just thinking the same thing."

ELEVEN

GIL AWOKE Friday morning earlier than usual. He fixed himself some coffee and raisin English muffins and ate out on the balcony. He stared down over Clayton without seeing any of the people walking the streets on their way to work. It was obvious someone was trying to involve Claire in murder, if not frame her for the death of three women. But if they wanted to frame her, why weren't they leaving something more in the way of evidence at the scenes? Why just those videotapes?

Gil knew that if he was going to start poking around, he would have to cultivate one of the investigating detectives. The choice of which one was easy, since he now had an active dislike for Detective Myra Longfellow. He decided to call Jason Holliday and invite him to lunch. He did it right away, setting his half-eaten muffin and unfinished coffee down on the dining room table as he passed through on his way to the bedroom. He dug Holliday's card out from his wallet and dialed the number. To his pleasure and surprise, the man agreed, and they set the time for one o'clock and the place to be Fitz's, a restaurant down the block from Gil's bookstore.

FITZ'S WAS A BREWERY as well as a restaurant, but instead of alcoholic beverages, what they brewed was their own blend of soft drinks. Their cream soda was delicious, but the root beer was what they were most famous for, and it was carried in fast-food restaurants as well as supermarkets all over St. Louis.

Gil was first to arrive and arranged to have one of the oversized booths against the wall on the first level. He sat facing the door so he could catch Holliday's attention when he walked in. While he waited, he studied the stainless-steel brewing equipment visible behind a glass wall to his right.

Holliday spotted Gil immediately, as the lunch crowd was sparse that day. Making his way to the booth, the detective appeared almost melancholy as he sat down.

"You know," Holliday said, "my wife used to buy this stuff by the gallon, but in all my years in St. Louis, I've never eaten here."

"Used to buy? Is she...deceased?"

"Dead? Hell no. She, uh, moved out awhile back."

"Kids?"

He nodded. "One boy. She took him with her. Do you and your wife have kids?"

"From previous marriages," Gil said. "Claire has one boy; I have two."

"You see your kids much?"

"I see mine a couple of times a year. My ex took them to New York."

"How old?"

"Twenty and twelve."

"And Mrs. Hunt?"

"Her son, Paul, is twenty-three. He lives in Kansas City, works as a guide on one of those gangster-tour outfits."

"Ah," Holliday said thoughtfully.

A waitress came over then and Holliday took a quick look at the menu while Gil ordered a pasta dish.

"How's the meat loaf?" Holliday asked Gil.

"Well, my father always told me never to order meat loaf in a restaurant because you never know what they put in it. But he was definitely wrong when it comes to this meat loaf. It's great."

"With respect to your father, I think I'll try it. And a root beer," he told the waitress.

Gil ordered Boulevard pale ale but asked the waitress to please bring him a root beer with lunch.

"Well," Holliday said, folding his hands on the table, "this is nice. Suppose you tell me why we're here, Mr. Hunt."

"I wanted to talk to you."

"To me?" Holliday asked. "You mean, without my partner?"

"That's right."

"You don't like her much, do you?"

"No, I don't."

"Can't blame you," Holliday said. "She's hard to like."

Gil was surprised at the detective's candor. "Do you like her?"

"I never ask myself that about a partner," the man said, "but if you're gonna pin me down, I guess I'd have to say yeah, I like her—but I've got my own reasons."

"That's fine," Gil said, "and I've got mine, too."

Holliday thought a moment and then said, "Well, I guess it's not fair. I know your reasons, so you might as well know mine. See, besides being a good cop, she's the only woman I talk to now that I'm divorced—and the only woman who'll talk to me."

"I guess that means you don't date."

"Jeez, no," Holliday said. "Who wants a busted-down old cop like me?"

"I better not tell my wife that. She'd try to fix you up with one of her friends."

"Really? That might not be so bad...if they're as good-looking as she is. I hope you don't mind me saying that you're one lucky man, Mr. Hunt."

"I don't mind at all. But Claire has to stay out of jail if she's going to play matchmaker for you."

"So, that's what this is all about, huh?"

"That's what it's about." Gil leaned forward. "Big surprise, huh?"

"Not really," Holliday said as the waitress arrived with their drinks.

Gil hoisted his mug. "Here's to keeping my wife out of jail."

Holliday raised his glass. "I'll certainly drink to that. But then you're assuming that I want to put her in jail," he said, setting his glass down.

"Not really, but someone wants you to suspect her of those murders, or else why leave the tapes behind?"

"I really can't talk about the case too much, Mr. Hunt—"

"But that's why I asked you to lunch, Detective," Gil said, cutting him off. "To talk about it."

"I guess you're wasting your mon—you are paying for this, aren't you?"

Gil had to laugh. "Of course. I invited you."

"Well then, I guess you're wasting your money."

"Not really."

"What do you mean?"

"Talk to me off the record."

"You mean like a newspaperman?"

Gil nodded. "Yes."

"Why would I do that, Mr. Hunt? For lunch?"

"No," Gil said, "for justice."

Holliday sat back in the booth and stared at Gil for a moment. "You said that real well," he remarked finally, "with a straight face and everything."

"Okay," Gil admitted, "so it sounds corny."

"Let me ask you something, Mr. Hunt."

"We are sharing a meal, so I guess you can call me Gil."

"Fine, Gil, let me ask you this. Are you planning on playing detective?"

"No," Gil said, "I wouldn't call it that...exactly."

"Because if you are, I gotta tell you, it's not a very good idea," Holliday warned.

"Let me ask you something, Detective—"

"Hey, Gil, I think it would be okay if you called me Jason, or Jace. You are buying me lunch, after all."

"Jason," Gil asked, "do you think my wife killed those three women?"

"Truthfully," Holliday said, "I don't."

Gil heaved a sigh of relief.

"But I don't have any evidence, either way," the detective went on, "and I gotta tell you, my partner likes her for it."

"Jason, I can't just sit by and not do anything, you know?"

"I understand, Gil," Holliday said. "You love your wife, and you want to protect her."

"That's right."

"Look, if she's innocent and you start poking around, there's a killer out there who might not like it. And if she's guilty—whether you know it or not—"

"I know she's not," Gil said, cutting him off. "There's no question about that."

"If you start messing in an active police investigation," Holliday warned, "you could get yourself in a lot of trouble."

"Not if you help me."

Holliday laughed. "Then *I* could get in a lot of trouble."

"Jason—"

The waitress came with their food and Holliday suggested, "Why don't we eat, Gil. We can talk about this after lunch."

"But—"

"I'd like to think it over while we eat," Holliday said. "Maybe we could talk about something else for a while. You like sports?"

TWELVE

THEY TALKED ABOUT sports and then about books. Holliday told Gil that he had been doing a lot more reading over the past eighteen months, since his wife left him.

"She found herself a man who paid more attention to her," Holliday went on, "a younger man—a lot younger. To tell you the truth, I don't know what he sees in her. Don't get me wrong—I married her and I loved her, but she was never a raving beauty. Now she's fifty and living with a guy twelve years younger than she is. I don't get it."

"I have the opposite situation," Gil said. "My ex-wife cheated on me with a man eighteen years older than she is. Now they're living together; she's working and he's retired. I'll never get that one. What could she possibly see in someone old enough to be her father? And on top of it, the guy looks like a pit bull."

They both shook their heads in confusion and had to laugh. Then Holliday said, "Well, you're doing pretty good now, and I'm getting more reading done. I've just started a book by this Tom Clancy guy...."

AFTER LUNCH, they had some coffee and got back to the subject that had brought them together.

"So, what do think about my advice, Gil?"

"I guess it's probably pretty good."

"But you're not gonna take it, are you?"

"I don't want to interfere with a police investigation, Jason, but I don't see any other way."

"You're gonna—what do they call it?—run afoul of my partner."

"Not if you run interference for me."

"I've known her a lot longer than I've known you, Gil," Holliday said. "Tell me why I should do that?"

"Because you don't think Claire's guilty, and because you want to find out who is."

"And you can find that out?" Holliday raised his eyebrows.

"Maybe I'll stumble over something," Gil said. "And if I do, I'll let you know."

"So...what do you want from me?"

"Just tell me about the three women. Who they were, what they did, what they had in common."

Holliday leaned back in his seat. "Those are pretty good questions. Maybe you're a natural-born detective, huh?"

"I'm sure you're probably more of one than I am, Jason. Why do I get the impression you're a lot shrewder than you make out?"

"Shrewd? Me? Don't go thinking I'm some kind of Columbo, Gil. Myra's the brains; I'm just the muscle."

"Uh-huh," Gil said, "right."

"Look, maybe I can answer a few questions without compromising the whole investigation—but just a few, mind you."

"That should be enough." Gil smiled his gratitude. "I'd really appreciate it—thanks."

Holliday suddenly seemed embarrassed. "Never mind, just start asking. You've got until I finish my coffee."

The waitress came and refilled their cups three times before they were finally done and Gil had most of the information he'd been after. He didn't want to push his luck by taking written notes, so he had to memorize most of it.

"There's something I want you to remember before we part company," Holliday said.

"What's that?"

"I'll deny I ever gave you any of this info."

"You don't have to worry. I won't tell anyone where I got it. I swear."

"Guess I'll have to trust you. Oh, one more thing, Gil."

"Yes?"

"You can't get involved in an active police investigation of a murder," Holliday said. "If you do, *you* could end up being the one in jail, and how would that help your wife?"

"But how can I—"

"Well," Holliday said thoughtfully, "there is the question of where those tapes of your wife's shows came from. I imagine there's material on there that is copyrighted?"

Gil knew anyone watching the *Home Mall* program was free to record any portion of it, but he understood what Holliday was suggesting.

"And," Holliday continued, "I'm sure her boss would be interested in finding out where the tapes came from."

"Sure he would," Gil said eagerly, "and it would only seem logical that I ask around."

"No conflict there with a police investigation that I can see," Holliday said with a shrug.

They left Fitz's together. Holliday had parked in the

adjoining lot; Gil had only to walk half a block to get back to his store.

"You'll have your wife call me when she returns?" Holliday asked.

"I will," Gil said, "I promise."

"And you'll get me some more of those Clancy books?"

"As many as I can."

"That Jack Ryan, he's a helluva character."

So are you, Jason Holliday, Gil thought as the detective walked to his car. So are you.

THIRTEEN

"WOULDN'T THAT BLOUSE look darling with my pink suit?" Judy Belmont glanced over her shoulder. "Well, Whitey, what do you think?"

"Give me a break—I'm tryin' to read."

"You're always reading."

"And you're always watchin' the goddamn TV."

"Well, it's certainly more company than you are."

The celebration of her twenty-first anniversary, last spring, had brought with it the realization that Judy Belmont had lived with Whitey one year longer than she had lived with her parents. And that meant she had spent the majority of her life being defined as a wife. To say anything had turned out the way she expected it to would be a lopsided exaggeration.

Oh, sure, they owned their own home, but not the Colonial she'd always dreamed of, down on Ladue Road. But then Whitey wasn't the doctor she'd hope to marry. She'd never had to work after saying "I do," but that wasn't because they had enough money to live comfortably, or even someone to help out a few days a week. No, Whitey was old-fashioned, believed his wife should be at home—with the kids. And, knock on wood, they did have two gorgeous girls—Gloria and Barbara Ann. (Whitey had insisted on naming them after his favorite songs.) But both girls were married now, living out of state; they had their own lives, populated with husbands, children, and in-laws.

Money problems had slowly eased up after Judy and Whitey had recuperated from the expense of two weddings. The house would be paid for in five more years. And for now, both were in good health, with many more anniversaries still ahead of them. Judy had hoped they would travel, maybe take a cruise. But Whitey had ten more years until he could retire, and while his wife's routine had drastically changed, his had not. So Judy Belmont occupied herself with Bible-study class on Wednesday nights, church on Sundays, and, when her friends weren't available for lunch, home shopping on TBN.

Sliding off the sofa to get herself a cup of coffee, she walked by her husband's chair and felt a smidgen of guilt in her stomach. Whitey *was* a good man. He never asked anything unreasonable of her. He never hit her, never cheated, drank, hardly ever swore, and almost never mentioned that she had gained twenty pounds during the past year. All her friends told her how very lucky she was to have a good man at home who loved her the way Whitey did. She supposed they were right—about the love part. He'd told her over and over that he wasn't the sentimental kind and she should know, just because he came home every night, how much he loved her. He shouldn't have to tell her.

"Can I get you something?" She rubbed his arm.

"No."

"What are you reading?"

He looked up at her, happy for the chance to discuss his book. "It's a biography of General Patton."

"Oh." She smiled. "George C. Scott."

"No, the real General Patton, not the actor." He looked back down at his book.

"Sorry."

Balancing her coffee, a plate covered with a slice of chocolate cake, a fork, and a napkin, she rushed back to her place on the sofa. Spread out in front of her on the coffee table was a pad of paper, a pen, and a card with her *Home Mall* membership number embossed on it. The cordless phone lay on the cushion next to her.

A menu came up, as it did at the top of each new hour. The next segment would be Household Helpers. One of the newer hosts came on. He was handsome, blond, somewhere in his late twenties, and wore those small kind of glasses they used to call "John Lennons." He looked so nice and tan in his light-colored suit; she wondered how many hours a day he worked out.

"Welcome back, I'm your host, Lane Allison. Today I've got something that'll blow you away."

Judy sat back to enjoy the program, and her cake.

"A three-in-one reading lamp. You got to see this to believe it. It's a must for anyone who reads."

Judy looked over at Whitey, then back at the set.

"This is our deluxe model; you'll find it in those high-end catalogs for double the price. It's the latest in modern technology. At first glance, it looks like a regular lamp sitting on a table, but watch this."

While the host demonstrated how the table collapsed and folded back into a new configuration, Judy decided against using the phone beside her and went to the bedroom to order the lamp as a surprise for her husband. His birthday would be in a few weeks, and if she charged the gift, she would have it in time.

"I'm sorry, Mrs. Belmont," the TBN operator said, "but your credit card has been denied."

"Wait a minute." She grabbed her purse from the dresser. "Try this one." She gave the operator her Visa number.

"Hold on while I check."

It took only a minute for the operator to return. "No, I'm sorry but that one has been denied also."

Judy Belmont couldn't understand. She'd always handled the family finances. "I know, how about if you put the lamp on the easy-payment plan? That way, you only need a third of the total amount now. Right?"

"Of course we can do that, Mrs. Belmont. Hold one moment."

Before she could figure out still another solution, just in case the last one didn't work, the operator was back.

"Everything's been approved. Item number two thirty-six four eighty-one, will be shipped to your South County address. You should be receiving that in seven to nine working days. Is there anything else I can help you with, Mrs. Belmont?"

"As a matter of fact, there is. I was wondering if you could send me an application for the TBN credit card."

"Of course, I'll have it in the mail to you today."

"All the operators there are always so nice."

"Thank you, Mrs. Belmont, but it's our customers who are the nice ones. Have a good day and enjoy your lamp."

"Oh, I will. Good-bye."

Judy hung up and hurried back into the living room before she was missed. Sipping her coffee, she found it difficult to sit still. "I know something you don't know," she said to her husband.

He studied the back of her bobbing head for a minute. "Uh-huh."

FOURTEEN

Rain had been coming down in heavy drops since she hit Springfield. Claire was usually glad for any excuse to visit her hometown of Chicago, but after talking to Gil the night before, she was anxious to get home.

The trip seemed to take forever. Road construction on I-55 slowed traffic, the rain caused her tires to skid occasionally, and because of all the talk shows, she couldn't even find any music on the radio. The black vinyl box containing tapes for the cassette player was somewhere on the floor in the back, but she didn't have the patience to struggle to find it. So she distracted herself by reading signs posted alongside the highway.

ILLINOIS, THE LAND OF LINCOLN. WHILE IN SPRINGFIELD VISIT THE HOME OF OUR SIXTEENTH PRESIDENT.

How many times had she visited the old Lincoln home? She tried taking a mental count. Three school trips, the time she and Frank took Paul there when he was eight, two book-buying trips with Gil, and once with Rose.

Claire thought about her mother-in-law with admiration. Coming to the United States when Gil was a child, working in a factory to support her two children after her divorce, she had been determined and confident her entire life. Rose had also taught Claire more about generosity and kindness than any of her own family members ever had.

Another sign, this one for Lincoln's tomb.

Claire wondered about foreign tourists. Did they travel to the small town of Springfield, Illinois, to tour the home of Abraham Lincoln and wonder how its citizens could pass by such an historical spot every day of their lives and be so nonchalant? Were they aware that Americans wondered how the Italians, for instance, could not marvel each and every day at the great art and architecture surrounding them? She supposed it was all in getting used to things. Getting numb to the beauty—the originality. Was it possible to get numb to anything?

As she sat in her air-conditioned car, the windows and doors tightly closed around her, she watched history roll by while she remained insulated. Yes, Claire supposed she had gotten used to her surroundings. But if she had grown indifferent to any aspect of her life, she had been abruptly awakened from her complacency when she had become involved in a murder investigation.

PULLING INTO her parking spot in the garage beneath the condo, Claire grabbed her small suitcase out of the trunk and headed for the elevator. The walk was a short one and yet she was uncomfortable, feeling unusually vulnerable. She hated the tension swelling inside her stomach and even the relief once the doors closed. She hated being so aware of her feelings.

She let herself in, knowing it was too early in the afternoon for Gil to be home. Kicking her shoes onto a small carpet by the front door, Claire was surprised to see a single rose lying on the floor. Picking it up, she held it to her nose and inhaled deeply, wondering why Gil had left it there.

She walked through the living room, then into the bathroom. There, on the vanity, was another rose. She picked it up and smiled, adding it to the one already in her hand.

As she walked into the kitchen, she couldn't help but notice two more roses arranged by the telephone. Gil knew her routine so well, it comforted her as well as prompted her to make a mental note to be more unpredictable in the future. Glancing at the answering machine, she was glad to see no messages waiting to be answered.

Three more roses were strewn down the hallway. As she walked to the bedroom, she bent to pick up each blossom, giggling to herself. On the nightstand beside the bed was a vase containing seven more roses; a card had been propped up in front of the bouquet: "It's no fun here without you. I missed you too much. Call me the minute you get home. Love, Gil."

After adding the five roses in her hand to the others, Claire picked up the vase and headed for the living room, where she could see the flowers more frequently throughout the rest of her day. Standing back a little to admire the soft pink of the buds, and then the large end table, she thought how well she and Gil had blended not just their lives but their possessions together.

When they initially moved into the condo, four years ago, she had arrived with a truckload of leftover furniture from her first marriage and odds and ends accumulated during her postdivorce years. After unloading her things, they then drove the truck to Gil's small apartment in University City. How he hated that place.

Jill and he had been having a difficult time keeping their marriage together. As far as Gil was concerned, a separation was imminent. When he returned from a business trip, however, he found the real estate section on his desk, with three apartment listings circled in red. Not quite as surprised as he thought he'd be and more relieved than he'd expected, he called the first number and rented the apartment without ever setting a foot inside.

After his divorce became final, the realization that his fourteen-year marriage was over triggered a six-month bout of depression and loneliness. Each week seemed to bring confirmation that he would never find happiness with another woman again. Slowly, Gil's concentration fixated on his sons and the bookstore. After awhile, he had almost convinced himself he was adjusted and maybe a little happy with his life—until he met Claire.

Looking back on it now, the three years spent living in that cramped, dingy one-bedroom apartment left Gil with nothing but bad memories. It seemed only natural he would give most everything belonging there to the Salvation Army. He had even told Claire that he had so few things he wanted to take with him that the job would be easily managed by just the two of them. But when they pulled the truck to the back of the apartment building and started loading boxes and boxes, and then more boxes of books, the space inside the rental truck quickly shrank.

After countless trips up countless stairs, with Claire complaining and Gil promising that next time they moved, professionals would be called in, they finally had the condo filled. Gil's contribution to the decor had been two lamps, three chairs, a desk, several paintings, and one small dresser crammed with clothes.

Their first year together had been one continual shopping spree. They replaced, refurnished, and relished in starting over. It was agreed the things they kept had to have only good memories attached, or they bought items ready to be imprinted with their newfound happiness. Now, four years later, the condo was an eclectic mix of new and worn—two separate lives incorporated into one. They collected art from their travels, and between Gil's love of books and Claire's passion for clothes, their closets were packed. As Claire surveyed the room, she still thought it looked more like the occupants had been together a lifetime instead of just a few short years.

Turning toward the phone to call Gil, Claire was startled when it rang. After four rings, the answering machine clicked on and Gil's voice announced that the Hunts were not at home right now. The beep sounded and Claire immediately recognized Stella's voice.

"Claire! Come on, you have to be home by now. Pick up!"

Claire grabbed the receiver. "I'm here."

"Thank God! I was going crazy. Gil's a doll, but he doesn't tell me all the details, like you do. So? How's my friend doin'?"

"Fine, as long as I was in Chicago. But the minute I parked the car, I started to hyperventilate."

"What you need is to get your mind off things. How about a movie?" Stella was more than a movie buff; even she had to agree when friends kidded that there hadn't been a movie made she didn't like. "Do you think Gil will let you out of his sight long enough for us to catch an early show and get something to eat?"

"He's at the store until nine tonight; I think he'll survive without me a few more hours."

Stella Bartlett had been Claire's closest friend for more than twenty years. The two had met at an auction that Claire was attending and that Stella had organized. They liked each other from the first bid.

"I'm so glad you're back, Claire; I was worried about you," Stella said.

"Thanks, but I'm fine. Why don't you check the movie times and I'll call Gil. I'll get right back to you."

"Okay. I think a comedy would do us some good, don't you?"

"Yeah, I sure could use a good laugh."

CLAIRE GOT GIL on the second ring. "You must have been sitting on top of the phone all day long, just pining away for me," she kidded.

"Not exactly. Stella just called. We figured you'd be home by now. But, hey, if you want to think of me as some pathetic soul just wasting away until you got home, that's okay. Us men know how you women need to feel superior."

Claire walked to a chair and got comfortable. "Gee, I call to thank you for the beautiful roses, and I get such abuse."

"Maybe you shouldn't be so quick to thank me."

"What do you mean?"

She could hear him moving in his creaky old chair and knew he was sitting in the back of the store at his desk. "Well, the flowers represent sort of a good news/bad news thing. The good news is that you're home. And for that, I am truly grateful."

"And…" She waited.

"The bad news? It isn't bad, really, as much as it is annoying."

"Gil, tell me what you're talking about."

"Go into the guest room."

Without questioning him further, she got up and walked down the hallway. Turning the corner, she flipped on the lights and saw the small bed piled with envelopes.

"Okay, what am I looking at, Gil?" she asked.

"Fan mail. I went down to the station and picked up all the letters delivered while you were gone. Then I got all the boxes of mail you'd answered and filed. I never realized how organized you are. I even found a few shoe boxes full of letters in the storage room. I think I got them all. Can you think of anyplace there might be more?"

"You mean you want me to gather more than five years' worth of fan mail together? All in one place?"

"Right. It came to me, after talking to Holliday, that we should start going back and seeing if maybe you'd corresponded with any of those three women. Maybe there's even something there from the killer himself."

"That's a great idea." Claire was anxious to get started. "You hear all the time about those weirdos writing the police, bragging about what they've done. But it'll have to wait until later tonight. I promised Stella I'd go to a movie and have dinner with her."

"Okay, then. It's exactly four-oh-eight. We'll synchronize our watches and meet back in the guest room at precisely nine-thirty to start organizing things."

She played along with him. "How will I recognize you?"

"I'll be the handsome guy, the one jumping for joy because he's so glad to see you."

FIFTEEN

SIFTING THROUGH the hundreds of letters Claire had received during her time with TBN took longer than they had anticipated. For every old letter they read, two new ones arrived at the station daily. News coverage of the three murders slowly worked itself from the front page to the third, but callers and fans continued sending their questions and support via the U.S. postal service, faxes, and E-mails.

Somewhere around the halfway point, when the pile of unread letters was the same size as the pile of those read, Claire realized she had never talked to any of the order operators. Unlike other shopping channels, which took orders electronically, TBN processed each order personally. A human being answered every phone call, assisting consumers with orders, complaints, and problems. Benjamin Thurman had learned, while still a boy in Texas, that a little bit of southern hospitality went a long way.

MILLIE WINTERS HAD started working the order desk the very first day the *Home Mall* program aired. Her family was raised, her husband retired. She had seen the ad in the paper and decided, on a whim, to go for an interview. When she got the job, she worked part-time, using the additional income to buy gifts for her grandchildren. A few years later, after her husband died, she increased her hours to full-time and now thought of TBN as her second home. She was intuitive as well as congenial, and Claire knew if anyone could detect a strange tone in a voice, it would be Millie.

"Tell me the procedure—from the minute you connect the call until you hang up," Claire said.

They were sitting in the break room, snacking on candy bars from the vending machine.

"I ask the caller for the item number and then their membership number. After that, we go through stuff like size, color, quantity. Lastly comes the shipping address. If there's time, I ask if they want to talk to the show host."

"Are there ever any customers who ask to speak to us? Before you get a chance to invite them?"

Millie picked at her Milky Way. "Occasionally—not very often. Most times, they're surprised and even shy about talking on the air."

"So, choosing callers to speak to us is purely random? There must be some voices that seem threatening or hostile, some that you don't feel right about asking."

"Oh, sure." The older woman nodded. "There were a few that got away from me, at first. It was so new, the shopping by TV and all, and I didn't have any experience. Remember the woman who talked so sweetly until she got on the air and then tried to shock you with those awful words?"

"It was hard to keep going after that one," Claire said.

"Who knew? But we learned together. And just look at us now. You're this confident television personality and I'm a polished professional. I can tell by the time I have their order taken if they'll be good on the air."

Claire wiped chocolate from her fingers. "Well, dear professional, how about regular customers? Even I have a few women I recognize by now, just by their voices. You certainly must know a lot more than I do."

"Sure. And they know me. Why, there's this one lady, calls every day. She's a widow like me, a real sweetheart. And then there's a middle-aged woman in Indiana, an invalid, does all her shopping—everything from makeup to Christmas presents—with us."

"Could you make me a list?" Claire asked anxiously.

"Course, honey. No problem."

"Millie, have you been questioned about this by anyone else?"

"Besides you? No."

"Not even the police or Mr. Thurman?"

Millie cocked her head. "No, and I've been wondering why. You know, it really gets my goat that everyone seems to forget, except for you, of course, that it's us, the people behind the scenes, who really know what's going on."

SIXTEEN

CLAIRE RETURNED HOME that evening to find Gil still going through the letters. He had moved the operation to the dining room table, which was covered completely by envelopes. As he sat, hunched over, totally engrossed in his reading, she watched him a minute before speaking. Gil was one of the few people she had ever known who seemed completely comfortable inside his body. His light blue T-shirt hung in soft folds; while he read, he unconsciously rubbed his beard with his left hand. The sight of him made her smile.

"Still at it, I see," she said, coming up behind him and wrapping her arms around him. She leaned over and kissed his neck.

He nuzzled her face. "Claire, did you know that some of your admirers are…a little odd?"

She laughed and kissed him again, this time on the mouth. "Not odd, sweetie, creative and, sometimes, very unique."

"Look." Gil dug for something on the cluttered table. Finding the picture, he held it up to her.

"What is that?" she asked, narrowing her eyes. "It looks like—"

"It is! It's a photo of a man's naked butt."

"Oh my God." She took it from him, holding it closer

for a better look. "It is…not nearly as cute as yours, though."

"Doesn't this worry you?" he asked, taking it back. "This is a letter and photo from some nut. Some nut who's out there, wanting you…wanting you to want him."

"Gil." She walked to the kitchen. Opening the refrigerator, she removed a small bottle of water. After unscrewing the cap, she took a sip, then stepped back into the dining room. "Honey, that's part of it—being in the public eye."

"I don't like this." Gil shook his head. "I'll have to talk to Thurman about security at the station."

"We have security."

"Oh yeah, that old guy—what's his name?—the one who's always asleep."

"Nate is sweet."

"That may be," Gil said, "but you need security, not only because of nuts like the Butt Man here but also because of this whole murder situation. I don't know why I didn't think of it before. You could be in danger at the station. You hear about stuff like that happening all the time, right in broad daylight."

She hated to admit it, but she agreed with him. "I hadn't thought of it, either. I'll talk to Thurman tomorrow."

Gil tossed the photo and accompanying letter—he didn't dare remind her what it said—into the trash can.

"Gee, looking at all this mail makes me feel like a real celebrity."

"Or a prisoner."

"What?"

"Some of these are like the letters men and women

get in prison," he said. "There are at least half a dozen proposals of marriage in here."

"With photos?"

"More like portfolios."

"Ooh, Gil," she teased, "I'll have to save those to keep you in line."

"And you have hundreds of female fans—"

"Well," she interrupted him, "that's my target audience."

"I especially like the picture of the lady with her twelve cats, each one of them dressed in matching hats."

"I bet that was sent when we did Craft Day."

"Here's one from a woman. It's postmarked about eight weeks ago," he said, holding it out. "Apparently, she's wearing something she bought from you."

"You mean from the station?" Claire accepted the photo.

"From you. She makes it very clear in her letter that she bought the item based on your enthusiastic recommendation."

"Oh, that beautiful diamond and ruby choker. I love that piece."

Gil sat back. "Look past the necklace."

Claire sipped her water again and frowned at the photo. "Past the chok—oh, you mean at the woman? Why, do we—oh…oh my."

Gil watched as she placed the bottle down on the table without looking. If he hadn't moved so quickly, it would have tipped over and soaked some of the letters. He caught it and righted it while Claire continued to stare at the photo in horror.

"Gil," she said, "that's—is that—it is, isn't it? It's her!"

"It's her all right. Mary Dunn, the second woman to get murdered."

"I remember her now!" Claire exclaimed.

"The envelope had already been opened. This must be one of the letters you did read, and when the police showed you another photo of her, you remembered."

"No—I mean yes, you're right, but that's not what I meant. I remember talking to her on the phone. She was very...sweet."

"So is her letter."

She sat down opposite him, heavily, still clutching the picture in her hand. "What's happening, Gil? Am I to blame for this somehow?"

He reached across the table and took her hand. "That's not even an option, sweetheart, so put it out of your mind."

Claire laid the photo down and looked at the sea of paper spread out in front of her. "Is there—are the other victims here?"

"I don't know," he said softly, "not that I've seen, yet."

Gil assumed she'd lost interest in the water, so he stood up, walked into the kitchen, and put it back in the refrigerator.

"What did you do today?" he asked her.

"What? Oh, I talked to some of the operators. Millie Winters was helpful."

"I like Millie."

"And she likes you."

"Of course," he said with false modesty, "all women do."

"Don't I know it." She knew he was trying to get a laugh out of her, but it just wouldn't come.

"So, tell me," he said sitting opposite her again, "what'd Millie say?"

Claire related her conversation to him as accurately as she could get it. She was like that. She'd try to repeat a conversation, any conversation, exactly as she'd heard it. She always had to start a few steps back, describing the setting as well as what the participants wore. It had driven Gil crazy the first year they were married, but it quickly became apparent that rushing her had not been the way to go. In the end, he learned that her versions of conversations were almost as accurate as tape recordings, and he listened attentively.

"So she gave you a list?"

"Yes."

"Well, that's great," he said. "We can compare that list of regular customers to these letters—wait a minute."

She smiled. "Now you're thinking what I'm thinking."

"Which is?"

"You're wondering if the names of the murdered women are on the list?"

"Well? Are they?"

"I didn't have time to read the whole thing. After going off the air, I came right home. I wanted to do this with you."

"Ah, you're such a romantic. Well, let's have a look."

SEVENTEEN

THEY SPENT HOURS together, pouring over the letters and photographs. Every so often, one of them would find something worth commenting on and they'd pause to study it. When they would finally determine the letter meant nothing, they'd return to the task at hand. Several hours had gone by when they both looked at each other and realized they were hungry. Pausing only long enough to order a pizza, they continued reading until it was delivered.

Eating in the living room seemed easier than trying to maneuver around the stacks of opened and unopened letters. Taking a break in front of the television, they watched the news in silence, each hoping another victim had not been claimed.

When they were finished, the leftovers were set aside and Gil and Claire returned to their places. It was almost midnight when they read the last piece of correspondence.

"Nothing," Claire said. "The other two women aren't here. I don't know whether to be happy or sad."

"Since Millie wants to be so helpful," Gil said, "ask her about the women by name tomorrow. See if she recognizes any of them."

"I'll do that." She stretched and caught her husband watching her. "What?"

"I'm just reminded every so often how much I love you."

"And what was it that reminded you now?"

"I like the way you move, and I especially like that little thing you do with your head."

She gave him an exasperated look. He had been telling her since they had met that she did "this little thing" with her head. Just a little unconscious movement that he liked but had never been able to duplicate for her.

"Not that again."

He just smiled.

"I'm going to get ready for bed," she said.

"I'll make some tea."

"That sounds good." She liked nothing better than to curl up on the sofa in her pajamas and have tea and cookies with him at night. Usually, they watched some old rerun on TV together. She thought again—as she had so often since they'd met—how well suited they were for each other.

While she went into her bathroom and got undressed, he went into the kitchen to prepare the tea. He was pleased to find some chocolate-chip cookies—Claire's favorite. He hoped they would take her mind off the murders for a while. He was saddened that she would ever think she was responsible, in some way, for the deaths of those women. He was also angered that, apparently, there was someone out there who wanted to implicate her.

Tonight, he heated the water in a pan, rather than in the microwave, so the tea would be good and hot, the way she liked it. He took out one of their best plates and arranged some cookies on it. After the tea had steeped, he carried her favorite mug and the cookies into the living room, setting them down on the coffee table in front of the sofa, on the left side. She always sat on that side, while he sat on the right. Sometimes at night, after dealing with people all day, they each wanted their own space. But as the evening wore on, she'd stretch her feet out to touch him, or he'd scoot to her side, or she'd lean over, resting her head on his shoulder. Invariably, all this touching led to bed and that—depending on how tiring a day it had been—lead to either sex or sleep. While they loved each other more and more with each passing day, sex had become something that occurred when real life didn't get in the way. But when things overwhelmed them, they'd go away for a few days, where all they had to concentrate on was each other.

As he carried his own tea to the coffee table, he thought that they were going to need something longer than two or three days when this was over.

When Claire came out and saw the tea and cookies, her heart melted. "You are so sweet," she said, sitting on the sofa and touching his arm. He leaned over and kissed her.

"What will it be tonight?" he asked. "A movie, or Bob?"

"Bob. I'm too tired to watch a whole movie."

"Newhart it is," he said, but he knew he'd have to wade through an *I Love Lucy* rerun first. He'd seen enough of those over the years to last a lifetime, but Claire seemed to be rediscovering them.

Settling back into the overstuffed cushions, Gil thought it really didn't matter what they watched as long as they watched it together.

EIGHTEEN

IN THE MORNING, while Claire got ready to go to the station, Gil decided to ride along with her.

"What about the store?"

"Don't worry about that," he said. "What's more important than the store?"

She gave him a wide-eyed, innocent look, pointed to herself, and asked, "I am?"

"That's right, you are."

Claire wasn't scheduled to work that day, so they were making the trip specifically to talk to Thurman about security.

When they pulled into Claire's parking space at the station, she said, "I've thought about this all the way down here. I think I should go and talk to him alone."

"I agree."

"You do? Gee, I thought you'd argue with me."

"No," Gil said. "He's *your* boss, so you should talk to him about this."

"And what will you do? Stand around and chat with the models?"

"No. I thought I'd talk to Millie."

"That's a good idea," she said. "Maybe she'll remember something else. Put on that 'little boy lost' routine." She held the door open for him. "You know, the one that makes women drop everything to help you."

He winked at her. "What makes you think it's an act?"

Gil waited while Claire went up the stairs to Thurman's office. When she was out of sight, he walked over to where the telephone operators sat.

"Gil!" Millie greeted him enthusiastically. She removed her headphones to talk to him. "How are you?"

"I'm fine, Millie. How are you?" He held her hand gently in both of his.

"Oh, same old, same old. What are you doing here? Don't tell me that wife of yours let you out alone."

"No, Claire's upstairs talking to Mr. Thurman. I just thought I'd drive in with her and make her buy me lunch. I also wanted to talk to you. Can you take a break?"

"Is this about…you know…what's going on?" Millie lowered her voice to a conspiratorial whisper.

He lowered his voice as well and said, "Yes, it is."

She set the headphones down. "I can take a few minutes."

He followed her to a room where she and the other employees took their breaks. The territory was totally unfamiliar to him. There were vending machines against one wall for soda, coffee, chips, candy, and sandwiches. A microwave oven, refrigerator, and sink lined the opposite wall. Chairs and tables filled in the center of the brightly lit room.

"Do you want anything, Gil?" she asked.

"No, Millie, thanks."

"I'm going to have a cup of coffee."

Gil moved quickly. "Let me get that for you," he said, dropping in the proper amount of change.

"Thanks. Hate to rush you, but I only get fifteen minutes."

"I just have a few questions."

After they were seated, she blew on the hot drink and then said, "Shoot. That's what they say, right?" She smiled broadly.

"That's it," Gil agreed. "Millie, do you know any of these women?" He took out a small notebook and read off the names of the dead women.

"Sure."

"You do?"

She tapped her head and said, "I have a great memory."

"How many of them do you remember?"

"Just one."

"Which one?"

"The last name."

Gil checked his notes. "Susie Kennedy?"

"That's right."

"How do you know her?"

"She's a—was a customer."

Gil's heart started to beat faster. Finally, a connection! Mary Dunn and Susie Kennedy had both been customers of Claire's shopping program. "A good customer?"

"We've got three kinds of customers, Gil. Regular, occasional, and new."

"Which one was Susie Kennedy?"

"She was occasional."

"Then how come you remember her so well?"

Now Millie looked sheepish.

"Millie?"

"You won't tell, will you, Gil?"

"Tell who?"

"Mr. Thurman."

"I won't tell him, promise," he said, crossing his heart. "Exactly what is it I'm not telling him?"

"Well, when we take orders, we're not supposed to, you know, have real conversations with people. There's only so much time to take their name and process orders."

"But you had one with Susie Kennedy?"

"More than one."

"Why her?"

"We had a lot in common," Millie said. "We were both widows, we both worked, and we both—this part, you really can't tell, okay?"

"I swear."

"Oh, you don't have to swear, Gil. I'll just take your word for it."

"You have my word," he said patiently.

"Well, we both went to the boats."

"The boats," he repeated, and then added, "Oh, you mean the riverboats?"

"That's right."

There were at least half a dozen casinos within driving distance of St. Louis. Some were legitimate boats that made cruises up and down the river. A few were considered dockside gambling facilities. This meant they were built on the river, as dictated by the law, but were in buildings in no way resembling a boat.

"So, you both gambled?"

"Just the slots and a little roulette." Millie sipped her coffee, staring into the cup.

"And that's the part you don't want Thurman to know about?"

She looked up, then past him at the door. "No, I don't want you to tell him that we actually met. Just once."

"You and Susie Kennedy?"

Millie nodded. "We weren't friends. I mean, I'm sorry she's dead and all, but we weren't really friends.

We arranged to meet once out at Casino St. Charles, but she really wasn't my type, you know? I mean my type of friend.''

Gil ran a hand down the crease of his khakis. ''Why not?''

''Well, I like to gamble, but she *had* to gamble. Know what I mean?''

''She was compulsive?''

''That's it,'' Millie said, ''compulsive. She got real hyper about it, too. She was hard to be around, so I made sure we never met again. In fact, some of the other operators started taking her orders.''

''Millie, are you sure you don't recognize the name Mary Dunn?''

''No, I'm sorry, I don't.''

''She was apparently a regular customer.''

''She must not have been very friendly,'' Millie said. ''Maybe we just never talked beyond giving and taking her order.''

That was certainly possible, Gil conceded.

''I have to get back, Gil.''

''Sure, Millie, thanks a lot for talking to me.''

''I hope this helps Claire.'' Millie got to her feet. ''Everyone here just loves her.''

''I'm kinda fond of her myself.''

''Lucky girl.'' Millie patted Gil on the shoulder.

After she had left, he walked to the soda machine and got a diet Coke. He took it to a table and drank slowly, going over what Millie had told him and what he already knew.

Mary Dunn and Susie Kennedy were both customers of the *Home Mall,* where Claire worked. They knew this because Dunn had written to Claire and sent a photo, and because Millie had spoken to Susie Kennedy, even met her once. What they didn't know was whether or not the first woman, Kathleen Sands, had been a customer.

"There you are," Claire said, entering the room. "Millie told me you were in here."

"Want a Coke?" he asked.

"No. I want to leave."

"We can't yet."

"Why not?"

"I have to talk to Thurman."

"He's already agreed to extra security. Besides, I thought you said I should handle this by myself."

He finished his soda and dropped the can in a nearby trash container. "Just how firmly is he behind you on this?"

"One hundred percent, especially if it means publicity. Probably seventy-five or eighty percent if not, and less if it starts to hurt his station."

"Claire, we need access to his records," Gil said. "Specifically, we need to find out if Kathleen Sands was a customer."

"Millie told me she talked to you about Susie Kennedy."

"That's another reason we need Thurman's customer records," Gil said. "Susie Kennedy's address. We already have Mary Dunn's from her letter."

Claire stopped to think for a moment. "But can't the police give us those addresses? And if they won't cooperate, can't we just check the paper? Surely there was something in the obituaries."

"We don't want to get in the way of the police investigation. And if we go to check out newspaper accounts, we'll be tied up all day at the library. Why not get all the information now? While we're here? And with any luck, we might find out that Kathleen Sands was a customer and we'll have all three.''

"Okay, then what do we do?"

"We go and talk to their families."

"What would we ask them?"

"I haven't thought it through yet, but I do know we need to talk to as many people as possible to find out who's involving you in this. Now, will you take me up to see Thurman?"

"Of course," she said. "Come on."

"GIL." BENJAMIN THURMAN sighed. "I'm sure you realize that what you're asking me to do is unethical."

Thurman was seated behind his desk, while Gil and Claire were standing in front of it, double-teaming him.

"Ben," Claire asked, "haven't you ever done anything a little unethical in your life?"

"Well, of course I have. How do you think I got to be so damn rich? But I've always had a very good reason for everything I've done. What you're asking me to do is violate the trust of my viewers. People who trust me when I promise not to give away or sell their names to any other company. They shop with us because they trust us not to invade their privacy."

"But we're not asking you to violate the trust of any customers currently doing business with your station, and we certainly will not give out this information to anyone else."

Thurman chewed on the end of his unlit cigar, still not convinced.

"How about one very good reason for you to help us?" Gil asked.

"Which is?"

"To keep the police off Claire's back and out of your station."

Thurman stared at Gil for another ten seconds and then picked up his phone.

NINETEEN

WHEN WHITEY CAME home from work, he wasn't surprised to find his wife, Judy, sitting in front of the TV, watching the *Home Mall* show. He knew, without looking, that in front of her was a pad with item numbers written on it and next to that was the cordless phone.

"I'm home," he said.

She tore her eyes away from the screen just long enough to greet him. "Hello, dear. Your dinner is in the fridge. Just pop it in the microwave."

He had to give her credit. No matter what she did all day to occupy herself, his dinner was always ready to reheat. Sometimes he wondered why she didn't just buy frozen dinners and leave it at that.

"Ooh, God, I've got to have that," he heard her say as he walked down the hall to their bedroom. He wanted to wash up and change his clothes before eating.

While Whitey was out of the room, Judy wrote down the number of a teddy bear-print T-shirt. She had made note of five items in the past hour, but she knew there was only room on her credit card for one of them. Earlier that day, she'd drawn some cash out of the bank and mailed money orders to MasterCard and Visa, but the payments wouldn't get to them until next week. Luckily, Whitey didn't check the bank accounts. From the first day of their married life, it had been her job to manage the finances.

As she watched the hostess talk about the latest fashions, she thought how much better Claire Hunt was than any of the others. If she had her way, Claire would work all the time, but the poor dear did deserve a day off now and then, especially with everything that was going on. Judy shook her head at the idea of those women being killed, and poor Claire drawn into the whole ugly mess. What a coincidence that Judy had even known one of the victims. She and Susie Kennedy used to sit next to each other at the nickel slots in St. Charles, until the casino replaced the machines with quarter slots. After that, Judy didn't see Susie all that much. Maybe she had gone to a different casino—maybe that new one across the bridge. That place was supposed to be the biggest gambling complex in the Midwest, but they couldn't lure Judy away from St. Charles. She was loyal—at least when she was gambling.

Ever since she had discovered the *Home Mall* show, though, she'd cut back on her trips to the boats. Actually, it had been Whitey who had made her stop. After that story came out in the papers about the woman in West County who had gambled away all her family's money on one of the riverboats. She'd been going every day, spending hours in front of a video poker machine. After draining their savings accounts, all three of her children's college funds, and cashing in their life-insurance policies, she couldn't face what she had done. One night, she snapped, ran down into her basement, and shot herself in the head.

"That's it!" Whitey had said. "I ain't havin' you go down to the basement just because you can't control your habit."

"But we don't have a basement, dear," she'd reminded him.

"We don't have to have a basement for you to know what I mean. No more boats!"

He'd forbidden her to go to any casino anymore. That had been months ago, before she discovered the *Home Mall* and that angel Claire Hunt. Sometimes it seemed to her as if Claire were speaking directly to her. The other women in her Shopping Club felt the same way. They all loved Claire!

That reminded her. Picking up the phone, she called Louise, one of the women in her club. She had to tell her about the lace shell, two items ago—as if Louise wasn't also sitting in front of the TV.

When Whitey came back into the room, his wife was on the phone. He stood there long enough to determine she was talking to one of her girlfriends, and then he went into the kitchen to nuke his dinner.

TWENTY

ARMED WITH THE addresses of both Mary Dunn and Susie Kennedy. Gil and Claire decided to go to the Dunn residence first.

"Do we know if she had a husband?" Claire asked.

"No," Gil said, "I never asked."

"Neither did I."

Claire was driving her Tercel and Gil had the chance to watch buildings and highway foliage go by. They were on Highway 44. When they hooked up with I-55, they'd be going south, toward South County. Mary Dunn had lived in an apartment complex in Mehlville. Although this was not within the St. Louis city limits, Gil knew Detective Holliday and his partner, Longfellow, had ended up with the case because they were from the Major Case Squad, which handled all violent crimes in the St. Louis area, regardless of whether they took place in the city or county.

They took I-55 and got off at the Lindbergh Boulevard exit.

"We go right?" Claire asked.

"Left."

She made a face. Even though she knew her way around the city, something seemed to happen to her sense of direction whenever she was behind the wheel and Gil was in the passenger seat.

It took them several more wrong turns before they found the development. They circled the area for a while before finally finding the right building.

"I hate these complexes," Claire said, parking the car. "Whatever happened to neighborhoods? And front porches? No wonder people act like animals when they're caged up in these kinds of prison-type compounds. Square brick buildings, all in a row. A human being needs to live surrounded by nature; I haven't seen one tree around here. And look how the management put black numbers on top of the black trim over the doors. Don't you think they would have thought to use gold or silver?"

"It certainly would be easier to find people," Gil said, nodding as they got out of the car.

"I'm bitching, aren't I?"

"Just a little."

She buttoned up her suit jacket. "I'm nervous. What are we going to say to these people?"

"I don't know; guess we'll just have to wing it."

"You're better at that than I am."

"What are you talking about?" he asked. "You work in live television, in front of a camera, almost every day."

"That's different. I can be the wittiest, most charming person while I'm on the phone with some customer in Nashville, talking about her new quilt and matching pillow set. But I don't know even how to start asking someone face-to-face about a loved one they've lost."

"All right," he said, "you've convinced me. I'll do the talking."

"Thank you, Gil."

"You're welcome. Now let's do this, before I lose my nerve."

"Sam Spade," she said, "my hero."

Gil rolled his eyes as they walked up the steps to the door of the building. Once inside, they found themselves in a small hallway.

"Do we know the apartment number?" Claire whispered.

"No, but we can check the mailboxes."

They found the name Dunn on a battered set of eight small metal doors mounted low on a wall. The family they sought lived in apartment D, which turned out to be on the first floor in the back.

"Here we go," Gil said, and knocked. Trying to reassure Claire, he was surprised at his own nervousness.

When no one answered, Gil knocked again.

"There's a bell," Claire said, leaning on it. They heard the chimes inside. Gil wondered how he could have missed it.

Finally, somebody opened the door. It was a woman who appeared to be in her early forties. Her face was pale and drawn, which Gil and Claire attributed to grief.

"Can I help you?" she asked.

"Uh, Mrs.—Miss—Ms. Dunn?" Gil stammered.

In that moment, seeing her husband so ill at ease, Claire thought how much she loved him, and she felt a sudden protective, self-assured attitude come over her.

"I'm sorry, you want my sister. She's not—oh God—" She started to cry.

"No, no..." Gil began, not knowing how to proceed.

Stepping neatly into the lead, Claire said, "It's all right," and she put her arm around the woman's shoulders. "We know what happened to your sister Mary."

The woman wiped her eyes with her hands and asked, "Then why are you here?"

"We just want to talk to someone—a relative perhaps."

"What about?" Suddenly, the woman became suspicious. Stiffening, she pushed Claire away. "Who are you?"

"My name is Gil Hunt; this is my wife, Claire."

"Claire—"

"I work for TBN," Claire interjected.

The woman's eyes widened. "That shopping channel. Why, you're the one on the tape."

"That's right," Claire said.

"Miss Dunn—is it Dunn?"

"It's Mrs. Nolan," the woman said. "I'm...a widow. My husband died two years ago, and now...now my sister."

She seemed to wilt then, and Claire put her arm around the woman again.

"Maybe you better sit down. Come on." Claire guided her into the apartment.

Gil hesitated, then followed.

TWENTY-ONE

CLAIRE USHERED the woman to a long sofa covered with a crocheted afghan. Mrs. Nolan sat down heavily, her arms dangling between her legs, her shoulders slumped.

"I'm supposed to be cleaning up," she said to them, "but I'm having a...a hard time dealing with...with all of it."

Claire sat next to the woman. Gil looked around, spotted a rocking chair, and pulled it over to sit.

"We understand." Claire tried to comfort her.

The woman sniffled, then looked up at them each in turn. "W—why are you here?"

"To tell you the truth, Mrs. Nolan—"

"Bonnie," she told Gil, "just call me Bonnie."

Gil started again. "Bonnie, we're not sure why we're here."

"It's about those tapes, isn't it?"

"Well, yes," Gil said. "We'd like to find out how one of them ended up here—uh, in the apartment, when, uh..."

He took in the apartment while he stammered. It was small. They were obviously sitting in the living room, and from it he could see the kitchen, dining area, a small bathroom, and a doorway leading to what looked to be the only bedroom. In fact, he remembered seeing a sign when they had driven in that said the complex offered only one-and two-bedroom apartments.

Gil looked over at the television and noticed a VCR on top of it. Mary Dunn must have been sitting on this sofa when she was found.

"Mrs.—Bonnie, do you mind if we ask you a few questions?" he asked.

"Why aren't the police asking them?"

"Haven't you spoken with them already?"

"Well, yes," she said, "a man and an extremely unpleasant woman interviewed me."

Gil and Claire exchanged a meaningful glance before Gil said, "We just have some questions of our own."

"After all," Claire said, "it's me they're finding on those tapes at the site of the…killings."

Now Bonnie looked at Claire very closely. "My sister always liked you. She even wrote you a letter once."

Claire smiled. "I know; I still have it. She sent me a photo, too. She looked like a very nice person."

"She was. Kind and generous but so…lonely. She never married, or had children. After my husband died, we became very close again. She was my best friend when we were kids, but after I got married, we sort of…drifted apart."

"That happens," Claire said. "The focus of your life changes. Do you have children?"

She shook her head. "My husband and I were never able to conceive."

"I'm so sorry."

"You don't have to be," the woman said. "We were very happy for twenty-one years, until he…he passed away."

"How did he die, if I may ask?" Gil questioned.

"He just went to sleep one night…and never woke

up. They said it was a massive cerebral hemorrhage and he never knew what hit him. I suppose if it's your time to go, that's the best way. But then this happened to...to Mary. I can't bear the idea of her suffering.''

Hoping to divert her attention before she started to cry again, Gil asked, ''Bonnie, did Mary have any tapes of Claire?''

She looked puzzled. ''Why would you ask that?''

''Well, I was just wondering.''

Bonnie thought a moment and then said, ''Well, Mary did tell me that she would tape the *Home Mall* whenever she had to go out, or to the boat....''

Gil sat up straight and quickly asked, ''The riverboats?''

''To gamble?'' Claire asked.

''Well, she *did*, before she joined Gamblers Anonymous. She was hooked on those boats—not so much on gambling. She didn't play the lottery; she didn't play poker or go to Vegas or even Atlantic City. She just loved the boats.''

''Any one in particular?''

''No.'' Bonnie said. ''She alternated. Or if she felt hot at one boat, she'd keep going there until her streak broke.''

''Did she win much?''

Bonnie smiled a little smile, the kind someone gets when they recall a fond memory, and said, ''She didn't win much at all; she just liked to play. I finally got her to go to GA, but she quickly replaced gambling with television shopping.''

''The *Mall* show?'' Claire asked.

''That was local. She also shopped QVC and the Home Shopping Network—I'll tell you a secret if you won't tell anyone else.''

"We promise," Claire said.

Bonnie leaned forward. "Once or twice, she ordered something from the Spice Channel."

Gil and Claire looked at each other. The Spice Channel was a Pay-Per-View channel that offered semi-hardcore porn movies. In between the movies, they demonstrated and sold sexy lingerie, massage oils, and sexual paraphernalia.

"Do you know what that is?" Bonnie asked, lowering her voice.

"We know," Gil said. "Hey, to each his own."

"My sister certainly was old enough to do as she pleased; I never meant to imply otherwise." Bonnie sat back, folding her arms across her chest.

Claire didn't want the woman getting defensive before they were finished talking with her. "Bonnie, do you know the names of the other two women who were killed?"

"I read them in the newspaper," she said, "but no, not offhand."

Gil refreshed her memory, then asked, "Do you think your sister knew them?"

Bonnie thought a moment and shook her head. "I'm sorry, but I don't know. I can't remember her ever mentioning them."

"Was your sister...seeing anyone?" Gil asked. "Did she date?"

"Not very much. She had a gentleman she would go to dinner with every so often, an older gentleman."

"How much older?" Claire asked.

"Well...Mary was the elder one of us; she was forty-five. This man is...uh, sixty-eight, I think."

"Sixty-eight," Gil repeated.

"There was nothing sexual going on between them,"

Bonnie hurriedly added. "They were just friends. He usually called her, and he always paid. It worked for both of them."

"Could you tell us his name?"

"I could, but I don't know where he lives, or even his number. I looked in the phone book and called information, but I can't find him; maybe he doesn't live in St. Louis."

"Why were you trying?" Gil asked.

"I just thought he should know what…what happened."

"If you tell us his name," Gil said, "and we find him, we could make sure he knows."

"Well…all right. His name is Jack Buxton. That's really all I know about him."

Gil took out a small notebook and wrote the name down. When he was finished, he and Claire exchanged another glance. Without saying a word, he knew that neither of them had any more questions.

Then Gil thought of one.

"Bonnie, one last question. Was Mary afraid of anything the last time you saw her?"

"Afraid?"

"Did she say anything about being followed, or watched?"

"N-no, nothing like that…."

"When did you see her last?" Claire asked.

"Two days before she died. We went to a movie."

Claire looked at Gil and he stood up.

"Thank you so much for talking to us, Bonnie. Guess we should be going," Claire said, "so you can get back to…what you were doing."

Bonnie shrugged. "This is what I was doing. Just sitting here. I've come every day this week to clean up, and I end up sitting here, staring at the damned TV without even turning it on."

"That's not good for you, Bonnie," Claire said.

"I know that." She looked down at her hands. "I know that... I know it..."

When she wasn't looking back up at them, Gil moved toward the door and Claire reluctantly followed. Somehow, she felt she should stay with the woman. Gil took her hand and shook his head, and they left, closing the door softly behind them.

Outside in the parking lot, Gil said, "You can't help her, Claire."

"That poor woman. First her husband, and now her sister."

"Maybe...she has other relatives."

"Somehow I don't think so, Gil." She looked at her husband. "I just don't think so."

TWENTY-TWO

"WELL," CLAIRE SAID when they were back in the car, driving home, "that didn't go very well."

"It was the first time for us. We just have to learn from it."

"Learn what?"

"The subtle art of interrogation."

"Is that what we're doing? Interrogating people?"

"It's what we did just now, and we still have more to go."

Claire massaged her neck. "I don't know if I can talk to another grieving family member."

"I'll do it, then," Gil said. "Besides, you have a job."

"And you have a bookstore to run."

"I'm going to talk to Allyn and see if he can work more hours for a while."

"Gil—"

He stopped her. "Claire, we have to do this."

"But the police are investigating. Maybe we should just leave them to it. They are professionals, Gil, and remember what they say."

"All right, I'll bite. What do they say?"

She smiled. "Don't try this at home."

He knew what she was trying to do, but why couldn't she understand that he was scared, that he was only trying to protect her? "Do I have to remind you that at least one of the investigating officers wants you to be guilty of murder?"

"That woman, Longfellow. I wonder why she dislikes me?"

"I have no idea."

"And what about Holliday? He sure seems to like you."

"I'm going to get him some Tom Clancy novels."

"I'm serious."

"So am I," Gil said, "but I know what you mean. He's been very helpful, but how do we know his motives? Maybe he thinks he's giving us enough rope to hang ourselves. Maybe this is his way, and hers, of playing that old good cop/bad cop routine."

"I hadn't thought of that."

"We can only trust ourselves, Claire. We have to find out what's going on, and then we can turn it over to Holliday."

"Well, we better uncover something before all of this starts to affect my work," Claire said forlornly. "How can I go on TV and be friendly if I'm terrified someone is going to be killed because of me, or if I'll end up dead."

"Something keeps coming up," Gil said as Claire steered them onto I-55 north.

"What?"

"Your *Mall* program is not the only thing these women had in common."

"What else was there?"

"Two of them used to go to the riverboats."

Claire thought a moment. "Bonnie just told us about her sister, but how do you know—"

"Millie told me that Susie Kennedy went to St. Charles to play the slots."

"So we know that both women shopped the *Home Mall* and gambled on the boats."

Gil rubbed the course hairs on his chin. "Right."

"What about the other woman? The first victim?"

"Kathleen Sands? We don't know anything about her, yet."

"Yes we do," Claire said. "We know she didn't shop the *Mall*. Ben didn't have any records of her making a purchase or even calling in for a membership number."

"Right. So if we find out that she gambled, then that's what the three women had in common."

"Which means...nothing," Claire said, "because the police found tapes of me at the scene of all three crimes. So we're back to the beginning with each victim having *me* in common. What do the boats have to do with anything?"

"For now, we don't know," Gil said. "All we can do is keep looking, Claire, keep poking around; we'll eventually come up with something."

"Spenser does that, in the Robert B. Parker books," she said. "He keeps poking around."

"Yeah, until somebody tries to kill him."

She tightened her grip on the steering wheel. "Or until he kills them."

TWENTY-THREE

"COME ON," Stella Bartlett coaxed, "we'll have dinner at the buffet; I have a coupon-two for one-and then we can spend some money. I know that always makes *me* feel better."

It had been almost a week since Claire had gone with Gil to question Bonnie Nolan. During that time, they had tried finding Mary Dunn's friend Jack Buxton. Gil had just computerized his store's inventory, and after figuring out how to go on-line, had found a way to access phone directories covering every state. Starting with cities within a sixty-mile radius of St. Louis, so far he had found one Jack Buxton in Pacific, Missouri, and two in Collinsville, Illinois. Before attempting to contact any of the men, however, Gil and Claire had decided that Gil should check further to see just how many Jack Buxtons he could find. Aside from the thoroughness of the plan, it also afforded them both more time to decide what they would even say to the strangers out there. But a day into the search, Gil suddenly realized he should also be checking Johns as well as Jacks.

While Gil tried to keep his business in order and surf the Internet, Claire had worked four uneventful days in a row, but she was starting to feel anxious, as if she was waiting for that horrible other shoe to drop.

"Stella," Claire wailed in her best Marlon Brando voice.

"What did I do now?"

"Gave me a great idea, that's all. You'll never guess what a coincidence this is, you calling now, asking me to go out to St. Charles with you."

"No." She didn't try to hide her sarcasm. "If I heard from you once in awhile, I guess I'd know what you're talking about."

"Sorry. Gil and I have been kinda busy, you know."

Stella let out a loud sigh. "I know that; it's just that I get so worried about you, Claire. So when this envelope came from the Station Casino St. Charles, I thought it would be something fun for us to do and a chance for me to see you. Why don't we just go out there tonight... Gil can tag along, too."

"He's working on something at the store and tomorrow he's got to get things ready for a signing; John Lutz has a new book out."

"Oh, I liked that last one of his you lent me, *Dancing with the Dead.*"

"I knew you would."

Stella had been an actress in her twenties and early thirties. She had performed on Broadway in countless bit parts and tapped her way across stage in dozens of chorus lines. But when she turned thirty-five, she decided that the toll endless auditions and rejections had taken on her self-esteem just wasn't worth any of it. It didn't take her very long after that to pack up her scrapbooks and return to her hometown. Now she lived in a small house in Webster Groves, an area that looked as if it had inspired a Norman Rockwell painting. She kept in shape by taking aerobics classes and competing in ballroom dancing. She was vivacious, charming, and made her living organizing benefits for various groups in town as well as in New York.

Stella started again. "Okay, so you and I will drive over the bridge and try to break the bank. Call that adorable husband of yours and tell him I'm picking you up around six-thirty."

"But it's out of your way to come here."

"Forget it. Tonight, you're getting the royal treatment. I'll be your chauffeur, your bodyguard, your friend... whatever you need me to be."

Stella could always lift Claire's spirits. "Sounds great."

IT WAS A HOT, humid evening, so muggy that their clothes stuck to them as they walked toward the elevator in the parking garage. The air felt almost too heavy to breathe. It was typical weather for late spring in the St. Louis area.

Construction hammered on all around them. But once they entered the main lobby, Claire was surprised at the spaciousness and elegance. Directly across from the main doors was the entrance to the Feast buffet. A line snaked in front of it within a roped-off area. Located at the far end of the lobby was a more intimate restaurant, featuring steaks. To the right were escalators leading to and from the dockside casino.

While the women stood in line, Claire people-watched. She noticed that the majority of the crowd seemed to be made up of colorfully dressed senior citizens. A three-piece Dixieland band played "Bye, Bye, Blackbird" while a little girl no older than two danced in front of the clarinet player. Her delighted parents and grandparents applauded. The atmosphere felt more like a state fair than a gambling casino.

By the time they were third in line, Claire could see an entryway for the gambling boat, which ran parallel with the wall of the restaurant. Two security guards were checking the IDs of four young men.

After dinner, Stella and Claire got their boarding passes and waited in another line as a television screen electronically counted down the minutes until boarding began. By offering two separate gambling venues, forty-five minutes to board, and staggered boarding hours, patrons never had to wait longer than fifteen minutes.

A security guard opened the gate at precisely eight o'clock. People began pushing through a turnstile after an attendant tore off a portion of their passes. As they rode the escalator up, noise assaulted Claire's ears before she could even get a good look around. Bells and coins clanked; music blasted over speakers as it competed with the excited shouts of gamblers.

The long room was lined with banks of slot machines, the middle arranged with blackjack tables and roulette wheels. Cocktail waitresses in revealing black outfits glided among the crowd, their trays loaded with cups of soft drinks and beer. Change people pushed carts that reminded Claire, in a strange way, of ice cream men. There were jackpots being paid out, cameras snapping pictures of the respective winners. It was immediately evident why anyone entering the room would get caught up in all the excitement.

Stella had been to the boats several times but knew that Claire had only gambled in Las Vegas, so she instructed, "Be sure you give the cashier your pass each time you get change."

"Won't the machines take my money?"

"Not in Missouri they won't. You have to get casino tokens and then they mark off that amount on your pass.

That way, your gambling is limited to no more than five hundred dollars a session.''

"Gee, just five hundred?'' Claire rolled her eyes. ''But what if I wanted to spend more, couldn't I just use your pass? Or buy one from someone else?''

"Bad girl. You're not supposed to do that; it's against the law or something.''

They decided to split up when Stella spotted a Keno machine she claimed was calling her name. Claire wandered around a few minutes before giving a cashier a twenty-dollar bill in exchange for two rolls of quarter tokens.

"Good luck, now,'' the pretty blonde said.

"I think I'll need it,'' Claire joked.

There were so many different kinds of machines that it took Claire ten minutes to decide which one she wanted to play. Getting comfortable on the stool, she unwrapped her first roll of tokens and started playing a Wild Cherry slot. The red symbol paid off whether it landed directly on the line or above or below it. She didn't see how she could lose.

The simple rhythm of inserting a coin in a slot, pushing a spin button, waiting, and then repeating the sequence again and again calmed her. After ten minutes, she realized she had almost been in a trance and felt more relaxed than she had in weeks.

But no matter how complacent she became, she couldn't help notice the people around her. Down two stools, to her left, sat a large woman dressed in gray pants and matching sweatshirt. Out of the corner of her eye, Claire watched as the stranger rubbed a green rabbit's foot across the front of her machine before pulling the handle with such force that it shook the others in the row.

A man, sitting near the aisle, chewed on a cigar while talking to himself. Rings on each finger made his hands sparkle as he worked the Double Diamond machine. Claire could only make out a miniature gold horseshoe design on his index finger and a pair of dice studded with what looked to be rubies on his pinkie.

After another ten minutes, the money she thought would be impossible to lose was gone. Deciding she might have better luck playing poker, Claire pushed herself away from the stool. A large sign suspended from the ceiling pointed the way to the ladies' room, and remembering her mother's advice always to take advantage of a clean rest room, Claire went inside.

A poster was taped to the wall. It's bold red letters read KNOW WHEN TO STOP. Beneath that in smaller black type was a question: *Think you have a gambling problem?* At the very bottom, again in red, was a number for the local chapter of Gamblers Anonymous, urging the reader to CALL NOW—ALL INQUIRIES HELD IN STRICTEST CONFIDENCE. Claire wondered if she was staring at the same poster that had convinced Mary Dunn and Susie Kennedy to join.

Rummaging through her small purse for a pen, Claire quickly copied the phone number onto the back of a receipt she had kept for no good reason. She hoped that maybe this number could lead to some answers where at least two of the murdered victims were concerned.

Back out in the casino, Claire continued to search for that lucky poker machine that would send her home a winner. Commotion at the other end of the room, however, caught her attention first. Curiosity directed her toward the area, but it was the anxious crowd that pushed her along. It took her only a second to recognize Stella's shrill scream.

"I won! I can't believe it! Claire! Can someone page my girlfriend?"

"I'm here, Stell." Claire pushed to the front. "What happened?"

"Look!" Stella pointed to the blue screen on top of the Keno machine. "All six of my numbers came up, and with four quarters in, I get sixteen hundred dollars! Isn't it beautiful?"

The white light on top flashed and a bell rang; change people gathered to congratulate Stella. A white-haired security guard, accompanied by another change person, walked over to Stella and ceremoniously counted sixteen one-hundred-dollar bills into her hand. With each bill that hit her palm, Stella squealed with joy.

By the time all the people had lost interest and milled back to their spots, Stella grabbed Claire's arm. "Time to leave."

"But I didn't get to play all my money."

"Save it for next time or cash it in, but we have to leave now."

Claire was confused. "Why? What's the hurry? You act like you did something illegal."

"No." Stella quickly walked Claire toward the escalator. "It is a wise man who knows his limitations. And I know that if we stay, I'll play back my winnings."

Claire could see there was no sense in debating the issue of willpower, so she stopped at the cashier's booth just long enough to trade in her roll of tokens in exchange for ten dollars.

Stella was so excited that she never noticed Claire had left her side for the moment. But by the time she was pushing the main door open, it was evident she was alone.

Seeing Claire running to catch up, she asked, "Where'd you go?"

"You're in such a fog!"

"Sorry. Come on, I'll buy you a drink. Hell, I'll buy you two."

"Anything as long as it's cold," Claire said as they stepped out into the humidity.

The wooden covered walkway leading back to the parking garage looked temporary, as though it had been thrown up until the real one was finished. Bright lights blazed against the white-painted surface; pictures and potted plants were arranged at even intervals the entire length. Claire stepped up to inspect one of the frames, looking closely at what it displayed.

"Those are the big winners," Stella said. "If I'd played the dollar machine, I'd be hangin' out here with the greats."

Claire read the name beneath the picture out loud. "Rosemary Johns, Arnold, Missouri, ten thousand dollars."

Stella stopped to have a look. "A dollar red-white-and-blue machine. Those are always hitting."

Claire walked to the next photo. "Here's a man in front of a Wild Cherry machine."

Stella read this time: "Fred Warner, St. Louis, Missouri, twenty-five thousand dollars."

They were almost to the garage elevator when they stopped to study the last photo on the long wooden wall. Stella read, "Kathleen Sands, Soulard, Missouri, twelve thousand dollars."

Both women froze.

"Could that be *your* Kathleen Sands?" Stella asked.

Claire stared at the picture without answering.

"Well, not *your* Katherine Sands, but you know what I mean."

"I wonder."

Stella reached into her purse and pulled out a gadget that looked like a combination screwdriver, bottle opener, and nail clippers. "Is anyone coming?"

"What are you doing?" Claire asked, amazed.

"Getting some proof for you to take to the police."

"But isn't that—"

"Vandalism? Yeah, so what? With all that's going on in your life right now, you're worried about borrowing a tacky picture that no one will miss?"

TWENTY-FOUR

GIL TAPED THE NOTE to the answering machine. He knew Claire's routine, that she always checked for messages the minute she walked through the front door. He stood back and read out loud. "Claire, I found Jack Buxton. He lives in Kimmswick; we're meeting halfway. I should be home early. Don't worry. Love you to pieces, Me."

Gil still couldn't believe his luck. Not only had he found Jack Buxton on the second call he made but the man had been more than willing to talk about Mary Dunn. While they went back and forth, trying to arrange a meeting time agreeable to both, Gil was surprised when the older man suggested they meet that very evening.

"I don't sleep much these days. Too damn hot" was Buxton's reply to Gil's concern that maybe it was too late. "Fact of the matter is, I'm a night person. Good thing, too. The sun'll kill you."

Gil couldn't tell from the man's tone if he was aware of what had happened to Mary Dunn or not, but why else would he have agreed to meet? He'd have to wait until he looked directly into the man's face to know for sure.

APPLEBEES WAS a family restaurant/bar chain. There were hundreds of them scattered throughout the Midwest. Decorated with sports and movie memorabilia or collectibles, they stayed open until 1:00 a.m. on weeknights and later on weekends. The crowd was usually made up of young married couples with or without small children and, in the bar, yuppies stopping in for happy hour or couples on dates. Their specialty was barbecued riblets, and Gil's stomach growled at the thought of the tender meat. A good eater with more than a healthy appetite, it wasn't like him to miss a meal opportunity.

While he drove, he popped in a cassette and harmonized with the latest Wynona hit. Claire loved almost any kind of music but could not understand her husband's fondness for all the country-western songs that, these days, seemed to be considered mainstream.

The setting sun streaked the sky with pinks and oranges. He thought about traveling with Claire to Ireland for a month when all this horrible murder business was over. He'd always wanted to see the thoroughbred racetracks there, compare the green of their fields with those in Missouri.

A thin elderly man, dressed in a crisp white shirt, waved as Gil surveyed the restaurant. He was seated at a table on the upper level.

"Good thing you mentioned having a beard," Buxton said, "or I'd never have spotted you."

Gil extended his hand. "Nice to meet you, Jack."

"Same here, Gil, although I'm not quite sure if I should be."

Gil slid his chair closer, careful not to hit his head on the heavy Tiffany lamp suspended over the center of the table. "Like I said on the phone, I wanted to talk to you about Mary."

A perky waitress dressed in a purple polo shirt and

black shorts approached. "Hi, my name's Cindy; I'll be your server. Can I take your drink orders while you look at the menu, or are you ready to order?"

"You did say we'd be eating, didn't you?" Jack seemed more interested in the menu than the stranger across the table from him.

"Anything you want." Gil smiled. "My treat, of course."

The old man's pale blue eyes lit up as he ordered a full meal, taking great care in asking the waitress to please bring his salad (extra dressing on the side) with the main course. After he was finished and Gil had ordered riblets and a Killian's Red, Jack watched appreciatively as the attractive teenager walked away from them.

Gil faked a cough to get the man's attention.

"Oh, I'm sorry. You were saying?"

"I believe Mary Dunn was a friend of yours?"

"Yes, yes she was. It was a terrible shock seeing the report in the newspaper that way, not to mention the TV coverage." He paused a moment, then said, "Poor Mary."

"Oh, then you know she's dead," Gil said, relieved that he didn't have to break the news to the man. "I was wondering…"

The waitress arrived with their drinks—Buxton had ordered iced tea—and once again the older man was distracted. Gil took the time to study him then. He looked pretty damned good for sixty-eight. He could easily have been ten years younger. He kept himself clean and fit. Claire was always commenting how some older men let themselves go, while others took excellent care of themselves. It was no secret the kind of old man she wanted Gil to be, when the time came.

"So tell me, Gil," Buxton said, "just why are you buying me dinner?"

"Jack…whoever killed Mary and the other women left tapes of my wife's TV show in their VCRs."

"Your wife's in TV? What's her name? Have I heard of her?"

"Claire Hunt. She's a hostess on the *Home Mall* program on TBN."

"TV shopping? Mary loved that show. Sometimes she even watched it while we were in bed—after we had done the deed, of course."

Gil stared at Buxton for a moment, remembering that Bonnie Nolan had said there was nothing sexual about her sister's relationship with this man.

"I'm sorry," Gil said, "did you say you went to bed with Mary?"

"Oh, yes. Well, I suppose you think it strange that Mary would be turned on by an old fart like me. Actually, I'm still quite…active in that area. A man my age, however, has to be choosy about his partners, what with all the diseases going around. Mary fit into my life quite nicely."

Well, Gil supposed that a man in his sixties could have sex several times a month.

"And she never conflicted with the others."

"Others?"

"Yes," Buxton said.

"Several women? Several times a month?"

"I suppose that doesn't seem like much to a young man like you, but it was satisfactory for me. And for the ladies, I hope."

The waitress appeared then and asked, "Who had the riblets?"

"Oh, uh," Gil stammered, still stunned by Buxton's announcement, "that, uh, that would be, uh, me."

"Then you're the steak." She placed the large plate in front of the older man, setting his salad down as well. "Can I bring you gentlemen anything else?"

"No, we're fine, aren't we, Gil?"

"Yes. Fine."

As she left, Buxton repositioned his plates and said to Gil, "It's just an old habit of mine, eating my salad with my meal instead of before it."

Gil picked up a riblet with his fingers and bit into it. He decided to forget about Buxton's sex life and continue with his questions.

"Jack, because of the tapes left at the scene, Claire's the main focus of the police's attention. I was hoping you might be able to tell me something about Mary that I could pass on to them. Anything. Frankly, I'm scared to death of what might happen to her."

"Well, Gil, I surely do understand. I surely do. Why, if I were in your shoes, I'd do the same thing for my wife...if she were still alive. God, how I loved that woman. No one woman could ever replace her, and she's been dead many years now."

"Will you help me, then?"

"I'll try, Gil," Buxton said, smiling, "because I trust you. Maybe it's the look in your eyes when you talk about your wife, but I know you're good people." He speared a tomato, then a piece of meat, and popped the whole thing into his mouth. "Ask away."

"What did Mary like to do besides watch home shopping...and go out with you, uh, several times a month?"

"The operative word here, Gil, is *shopping*. She loved it, no matter how she got it done. Formed a club with some of her lady friends—called themselves the Shopping Fools. When there was a holiday coming up, about five or six of them would take off for Chicago or Kansas City. Once they even flew out to L.A. They'd get a nice hotel and go shopping for days, eight hours at a stretch. They shopped Rodeo Drive, Beverly Hills, the Mall of the Americas in Minneapolis, Michigan Avenue, Country Club Plaza. Then they'd come home all happy with themselves, their suitcases bulging.''

"Did Mary belong to any other organizations?"

"I guess it won't matter if I tell you now, with her gone, but yes, she belonged to Gamblers Anonymous. She dearly loved those riverboats. So do I, but I had to find someone else to go with once Mary told me she had a problem. Pity, too, she was so intelligent. Loved the theater, concerts, art museums. Just couldn't control herself when it came to those casinos.''

Just as they were about to leave, Gil asked one last question.

"Jack, was Mary seeing any other men?"

"No.''

"You're sure?"

"I'm positive," Buxton said. "None of my ladies are seeing other men.''

Gil couldn't be sure if this was true or just wishful thinking on Buxton's part.

"I give them all they need whenever they need it. They want someone to go to the movies with, someone to lie with every once in awhile, and then they go on with their lives. That's how it was with Mary. You see, they're all in their forties, or early fifties; they're not looking for a home or children. Some of them had that. And most of them value their time alone. It's just that, once in awhile, they need someone.''

It made sense, the way Buxton explained it. But Gil

couldn't help wonder what Claire's reaction would be when he told her about it.

Gil paid the bill and he and Buxton walked out to the parking lot together.

"I hope I was of some help to you and your wife. Maybe you could call me and let me know what happens? I'd be interested in the details."

"Of course I could do that," Gil said. "And, Jack?"

The old man looked up at Gil. "Yes?"

"Thank you."

Buxton nodded and patted Gil on the arm.

Gil watched the man drive away, then got into his car, thinking about Claire, missing her. He was suddenly anxious to get home.

TWENTY-FIVE

CLAIRE DIDN'T LIKE Myra Longfellow. She hadn't from the start and now, sitting in the straight wooden chair next to Longfellow's desk, she still didn't. Claire knew the detective was deliberately making her wait—squirm. It certainly wasn't a secret that the woman thought Claire was guilty; everything about her said so. Her cold stare, her body language Claire had noticed it all and remembered it, but she still agreed when Gil suggested she go to the detective with their progress.

He'd brought up the subject after returning from Applebees, she from St. Charles, and they had compared notes.

"Woman to woman, you know, maybe you can win her over," he had said, trying to convince her. "After all, I've bonded with *my* detective."

"You don't have to give me any more reasons. I've been thinking the same thing—but I don't have to go happily, and I certainly don't expect to bond with her."

Claire checked her watch again. Another ten minutes had gone by, making Ms. Longfellow now twenty-five minutes late for their appointment.

The female detective had not agreed readily to the meeting. "What could we possibly have to talk about, Mrs. Hunt?" Unspoken at the end of that sentence was, Unless you want to confess.

Claire had taken a deep breath and said, "I think we got off on the wrong foot, Detective, and I think I have some information that might interest you."

In the end, Longfellow had agreed, but she had made the entire matter sound like a dreaded chore.

Claire looked around for the obligatory two-way mirror she'd seen thousands of times in cop shows, but there was none, just drab green walls and gunmetal gray desks. She could smell coffee and noticed an empty doughnut box in a nearby wastebasket. Massaging her neck she thought, Okay, I can wait just as long as you can.

When Longfellow finally did show up, she had a cup of coffee in each hand. Extending one to Claire, she asked, "Do you take cream or sugar?"

"Sugar."

The woman walked around and sat at her desk, opened the middle drawer, and pulled out two packets of sugar. Probably swiped from some restaurant, Claire thought.

Longfellow sat back in her creaky armchair and let out a bored sigh. "Now, Mrs. Hunt, what can I do for you?"

Claire definitely did not like this woman. Deciding to return the patronizing attitude, she tossed the picture of Kathleen Sands and a piece of paper printed with Jack Buxton's name, address, and phone number onto the desk. Then she sat back and stirred the sugar into her coffee with a red plastic stirrer.

Longfellow picked up the picture Stella had "borrowed." After studying it for a moment, she said, "A picture of the second victim, taken at a casino. What am I supposed to do with this?"

Putting her cup down, Claire folded her arms across

her chest. "Are you aware that two of the three women frequented riverboats in the area? That one of the three women had a problem and belonged to Gamblers Anonymous? That a visit to the GA meeting place might help solve this case?" Then Claire waited for the stone-faced woman to react in some way to the news.

But instead, Myra Longfellow folded her large hands on the top of her desk. "All *three* women belonged to GA, Mrs. Hunt. We've been putting in some time on this case, too, you know."

Claire refused to be deterred.

"Did you or your people know that Mary Dunn was seeing a man named Jack Buxton?" Claire slid the phone number closer to the detective. "And that Mr. Buxton told my husband that Mary belonged to a power-shopping club?"

"Which leads us back to you, doesn't it? If what you're telling me is that the common denominator here is shopping."

"For heaven's sake. Everybody shops! We live in a consumer-oriented society. Look around, Detective Longfellow, there's a strip mall on practically every corner; each city has some sort of galleria crammed with high-end stores. Why, there's even—"

"Home-shopping junkies?" Myra Longfellow finished.

Claire couldn't help herself and moved closer, bumping the detective's desk, causing some of her coffee to spill. Neither of them acknowledged it.

"We're a video catalog. People have been ordering from mail-order houses for more than a century now."

Longfellow seemed to enjoy seeing Claire's temper flare and said nothing.

"Look," Claire said, calming herself, "I just thought

we could work together on this thing. Isn't there always a manpower shortage in police departments? My husband and I are more than willing to cooperate in any way we can. I came here today to discuss our progress and maybe compare notes.''

Longfellow stared at Claire for a few moments before she finally spoke. ''Two things.'' She held up her index finger. ''Number one, if we did need help, we certainly wouldn't solicit or accept it from amateur detectives—especially one who is a suspect.'' She held up a second finger. ''Second, if you and your husband dare interfere with a police investigation, I'll see you both get some jail time, and some very bad publicity. Have I made myself clear, Mrs. Hunt?''

''Perfectly clear, Detective Longfellow.''

Claire stood and reached for the picture and piece of paper with Jack Buxton's information on it. Longfellow put her hand over the material.

''I'll just hold on to this for a while.''

''Fine,'' Claire said, turning to leave, then stopping. ''Oh, by the way.''

''Yes?''

''I like your shoes. I recognized our style number twenty-nine fifty-one immediately.'' With that, Claire marched out of the squad room.

Myra Longfellow sat frozen until she was certain Claire was out of the building. Then she crossed her feet at the ankles, scuffed them under her chair, and muttered, ''Bitch.''

TWENTY-SIX

"YOU'RE GOING TO pee in your bathrobe?"

Exasperated, Claire called out to Gil, who was in the living room, "No, I said I'm going to *be* in the *bathroom.*"

Gil had no problem interpreting Claire's body language when she had walked through the front door, passed him, and walked down the hall toward their bedroom. She was definitely angry. And his strong sense of survival told him to sit tight until his wife was ready to talk.

When she finally did come out, she sat down on the sofa with Gil and glared straight ahead.

"Well?" he asked after a few minutes.

She looked at him incredulously and said, "You know what that bitch did? She kept the photo and Buxton's information after acting like none of it was important."

"She didn't want to trade information?"

"Trade? That would involve cooperating. No. She threatened me—well, us—said we could go to jail if we interfered with her police investigation."

Gil leaned back into the cushions. "Didn't she appreciate anything we've done?"

"They knew most of it already. She said that all three women were in Gamblers Anonymous."

"Had they talked to the GA people at their meeting place?"

Claire reached for a handful of popcorn from a bowl Gil had been eating from. "I don't know."

"Did they already know about Buxton?"

She chewed angrily. "I don't know."

"Did they know about the power shopping?"

"Gil...darling...I...don't...know." She looked at him. "Why don't you call your good friend Holliday and ask him? After all, you two have bonded."

"Well, I just might do that, but not right now. For all we know, Longfellow may have had time to turn him against us, too."

"And you know what makes me even madder?"

"What?"

"She made remarks about home shopping while she was wearing a pair of *our* shoes! The woman shops with the *Mall* show."

"That explains how she recognized you on the tapes left in the murdered women's apartments."

"Gil," Claire said, "she kept me waiting for half an hour and then had the nerve to point her fingers at me like I was a bad little child she was trying to potty train."

"Well," he said with a sigh, "I guess that wasn't a very good idea. I'm sorry I made you go."

Claire couldn't help but laugh. "Aw, sweetheart, it's so cute that you think you could *make* me do anything. I hate to spoil your macho illusions, but it was my idea, too. I just didn't figure on meeting up with such a bull-headed human being."

"You, uh, didn't tell her about the letter and photo Mary Dunn sent you, did you?"

"God no! You think I want her believing I lied right

from the beginning and actually recognized a murder victim when they first showed me her picture?''

"You're a smart lady.''

She dropped a few kernels of popcorn back into the bowl and turned to face him with her body. The anger was starting to drain away and be replaced by—what—amazement—puzzlement?

"Do you honestly think she suspects me of killing those women? I never took it seriously until she called me a suspect.''

"When?''

"She said she wouldn't accept help from a couple of amateurs, especially when one of them is a suspect.''

"She called me an amateur?''

Claire's eyes widened. "She called *me* a suspect.''

"I know, I know,'' he said, "I was joking. Sorry.''

"I wish I could approach everything with humor, the way you do.''

"It's a defense mechanism with me,'' he said. "You know I'm just as scared as you are.''

"But you're scared for me from out there,'' she said. "It's different when I'm scared for me inside here.'' She tapped her heart.

"I know,'' he said, then amended it and began again. "No, maybe I don't, but I do know how terrified I am at the thought of anything bad happening to you while I'm powerless to help.''

She rested her cheek against the back of the sofa. Reaching out to touch his shoulder, she said, "So let's just do something to fix this.''

"Well,'' Gil said, "if they're going to be stubborn and not accept our help, then we'll just have to keep at it ourselves until we can prove to them how ridiculous their suspicions are.''

"How are we going to do that?" she asked. "We've been to Susie Kennedy's home and can't find any relative to question. What's our next move?"

"I'm glad you asked; I've been thinking about it all day. Gamblers Anonymous!" he said. "Didn't you take that number down when you saw the poster on the boat?"

"That's right, I did." She got up and walked to the dining room, where she had hung her purse on one of the chairs. She rummaged through it and came out with the slip of paper the number was on. Carrying it back to the sofa, she handed it to Gil.

"This is our only lead, now," Gil said. "I'll call and find out where the next meeting is. We'll go there and nose around, see if anyone knew Mary Dunn or either of the other women."

"When will you call?" she asked.

"Tomorrow."

She gave him that look that always worked on him, cocked her head, and said, "Call now?"

He smiled. "I'll call now."

TWENTY-SEVEN

ST. LOUIS IS KNOWN for having more than its share of churches, representing every denomination. It seems you can't drive a mile without seeing one.

The church Gil and Claire were looking for was on a street called Eddie and Park, on the corner of Sappington Road. As Gil pulled the car into the parking lot, he couldn't help but notice the large letters chiseled into the granite facade.

"The Church of the Persistent Dreamer," Claire read aloud. "I wonder what that means?"

"You got me," Gil said; unfastening his seat belt, "but for our purpose, it really doesn't matter, does it?"

"No, I guess not."

When Gil had called the Gamblers Anonymous number Claire had given him the night before, he'd been surprised twice. The first time came when he got a taped recording telling when and where the next GA meeting would be held. The second time occurred when he found out the meeting would take place the following day, at 5:00 p.m.

During the ride, Claire had asked, "Which one of us is the gambler in need of saving?"

"You are," Gil had said without one moment of hesitation.

"Why me?"

"You went to the boat with Stella the other night, didn't you?"

"So? You've been to Vegas, and racetracks."

"But I've never been on a boat," Gil said innocently. "You, at least, have had that experience. And haven't you seen those news stories about the floating dens of iniquity scattered up and down the river?"

"Every so often. Why?"

"Haven't you noticed they always do reports about women? I mean, you were there. You saw it all."

"I've noticed they like to sensationalize stories about housewives gambling. But when I was out with Stella, there were just as many men as women. Just as many baseball-capped, cigar-smoking men high-fiving one another every time the dealer laid down an ace in front of them," she said, irritated.

"Well, see there?" Gil said. "I didn't know any of that. You're the only one who can talk about the boats with any intelligence so that we can win these people over."

"All right," she finally agreed, "I'll be the gambler."

Now they got out of Gil's car and walked toward the church. "It can't be *in* the church," he commented.

"Maybe there's a parish hall, or a room downstairs?"

"A basement sounds right," Gil said, looking for windows. "That's where they usually hold bingo and stuff, isn't it?"

"I don't know."

"Well, you're supposed to know," he scolded her. "You're the gambler, remember?"

"Bingo?"

"When people go to AA, it's because they drink everything and anything. I imagine it's the same with GA."

"I guess."

"There, that looks like a stairway leading down." He pointed.

They walked toward it and Claire suddenly stopped. "Gil, what if someone recognizes me?"

Gil stopped next to his wife. "I hadn't thought of that."

It had happened to them enough times that it was a factor he should have considered.

"All right," he said, "looks like I'm the gambler."

She took his arm. "Don't worry, baby, I'll support you every step of the way while you fight this terrible addiction."

He stared at her and said, "You're good."

"I know."

They went down the steps.

JUDY BELMONT couldn't believe her eyes. There, across the room, was Claire Hunt. Obviously, the man she was with must have a problem, not Claire. For one tiny second, Judy thought of approaching Claire, but that thought was overwhelmed by her shyness. After all, the woman was a...a real celebrity. There was no way she could actually talk to her. She had even hung up the phone abruptly, several times, when the operators asked if she wanted to talk to the host. Judy just couldn't do it then, and she certainly couldn't do it now.

Suddenly, all she could think about was getting home and telling Whitey that she'd seen Claire Hunt in person.

"NOW WHAT DO we do?" Claire asked.

"I don't know," Gil replied. "We're the newcomers. Maybe we're just supposed to stand here and wait for someone to approach us."

As he said that, a pleasant-looking man in his early thirties, with black hair combed forward to cover a thinning crown, came up to them.

"Hello. You're new, aren't you?"

"Yes," Gil said, "this is my first meeting."

The man smiled broadly—beamed, in fact. "I'm Carlos Delgado; I'm in charge of things."

"Gil Hunt." It never occurred to him to use a phony name.

They shook hands and talked for a few moments. Gil was unable to detect any accent indicating whether the man was of Puerto Rican or Mexican descent; he obviously had spent many years in this county, if, in fact, he hadn't been born in the United States.

"Is this your wife?"

"Yes, Claire Hunt."

Delgado shook her hand, too.

"It's so nice to see you come with your husband, Mrs. Hunt. We don't get too much of that."

"Oh? Why not?"

"I think it's because by the time we're ready to come here—and I include myself—our spouses, or significant others, have just about had it with us."

"Oh," Claire said, taking Gil's arm possessively, "I would never turn my back on my man." She smiled then and kissed Gil softly on the cheek.

Delgado beamed again.

"With this kind of support, Gil, I don't think you'll have any problems kicking your addiction. What is your preference anyway? Cards? Horses?"

"Slot machines," Gil said. "Can't get enough of those...ol' one-armed bandits."

"Well, they're certainly easy to get to, aren't they?

With all the boats around here now? Although, I don't know why they call them boats.''

"Carlos?''

Delgado stopped and turned to look at the man next to him. He was slender, in his early to mid-twenties.

"Yes, Henry?''

"We're ready to start.''

"Ah, good,'' Delgado said. "Henry Wentworth, this is Mr. and Mrs. Hunt. Get them some coffee, please, and make them welcome. It's Mr. Hunt's first meeting.''

"Sure thing, Carlos.''

"I have to say a few words,'' Delgado said to them, "just to get things rolling. Since this is your first time, Gil, you can just sit, relax, and listen.''

"That's good.''

"Unless you have something you want to say, that is.''

"No,'' Gil said. "No, I think I'll wait.''

"That's fine. Henry will see to you.''

Delgado walked away and Claire turned to Henry.

"What happens now?''

"Carlos will speak to everyone, and then there will be some testimonials.''

"And after?''

"People will have coffee and cookies, or cake, and talk among themselves—ourselves.''

"Are you a…a member of GA, too?''

"Oh, yes,'' Henry said, "we all are—um, except you, I guess, Mrs. Hunt? Carlos did say it was Mr. Hunt's first meeting. Unless, of course, you've been to a meeting before?''

"Oh, no,'' she said. "I'm just here for moral support.''

"That's good," he said. "That's very good. Come." He pointed to a nearby table where refreshments had been set up. "We'll get you some coffee and then you can listen to Carlos. He's a very inspirational speaker."

TWENTY-EIGHT

GIL AND CLAIRE WAITED for Carlos Delgado's inspirational speech while sipping too strong black coffee from Styrofoam cups. But it never materialized. Gil found the man to be a most uninspiring speaker—although sincere enough—and yet when he was done, everyone applauded enthusiastically. Gil thought the man depended too much on his ultrawatt smile.

When he looked at Claire sitting next to him, he saw she wasn't listening. He could fill her in later, he thought, and turned his attention back to the microphone.

IT WAS CLAIRE who looked around and took in the different types of people in attendance. If women were doing most of the gambling in St. Louis, they apparently weren't coming here in droves. There seemed to be only twenty or so people to begin with and the mix seemed to be fifty-fifty. The group appeared to range in age from twenty-five to forty, and she wondered if that was because older people found having an addition too embarrassing; maybe they tried working it out by themselves. She herself had never had an addictive personality—well, to anything but her husband, Gil.

She also noticed—and felt slightly guilty for thinking so—that most of these people were not attractive. Once again trying to understand the addiction, she wondered if somehow gambling took the place of socializing in bars and clubs for them. Did it compensate for what was lacking in other parts of their lives?

There were some testimonials going on, but she wasn't listening to them. She knew Gil was, so she continued to study the group.

Several women appeared to be in the same age group as the dead woman. Mary Dunn was forty-five, and she'd been the oldest. Claire decided that, when the testimonials were over and everyone came to the table for their coffee, she'd engage these women in conversation and see what she could find out.

GIL WATCHED several people stand up to the microphone and listened while they stammered on about their particular addition. One woman talked about sitting at Keno machines for hours on end, pouring in her week's salary. Another man talked about the allure of live poker parlors on the boats. Still another spoke about his love affair with horse racing, which had gotten so out of control that he'd lost his job, house, and family.

If Gil had an addictive personality about anything—other than Claire—it was books. He'd once -had a huge collection—just another bone of contention with his ex-wife—but since opening the bookstore, he'd been able to satisfy himself with his stock, and he kept fewer and fewer books at home.

Nowadays, however, he actually preferred not to get involved in anything requiring him to be without Claire. Of course there were working hours, forcing them to be in separate locations. And when they were at home, they gave each other a few hours of solitude—an agreement they had made after the first six months of living together. But other than that, everything they enjoyed doing, they did together. Years ago, when he was in his twenties, even his early thirties, he might have thought such an arrangement stifling, but disappointments and regrets left behind from past relationships only made him more aware of what a wonderful thing he had found with his wife, and he was going to enjoy every second of it.

"Does anyone else want to speak?" Carlos Delgado called out. He looked directly at Gil, who did not react, for fear he'd actually be called upon. "Well then, help yourselves to refreshments. And mingle! Thanks for coming."

Gil was startled by Henry's voice, because the man seemed to have materialized suddenly and be speaking right into Gil's ear.

"What did you think?"

"It was…interesting."

"This is where we visit with one another, find out who shares the same problems," Henry said. "Excuse me."

"What *did* you think?" Claire asked.

"I'll tell you later," Gil said, realizing that twenty or so people were headed for the table he and Claire now stood in front of. "Mingle."

"Right."

PEOPLE PRACTICALLY RAN toward the refreshments, attacking the food like locusts. Gil wondered how many of them were really there for help and how many had come for the brownies and carrot cake.

Claire meant to talk to the women but soon found herself surrounded by men. She quickly realized they were looking at her as the new available female, so she politely pointed out her husband, confiding that he was the one with the gambling problem. This dissuaded all the men except one.

His name was Brad Trager, and he was tall, dark-haired, probably muscular most of his life, but getting a little potbelly now that he was in his early fifties. He still dressed like it was the sixties, with a floral shirt, the top three buttons open, revealing gray chest hair. He was so totally out of step with the times that he wore a white belt and matching white shoes. He was unmarried—or simply didn't wear a ring—and perpetually on the make. He made it very clear that her being married didn't matter to him.

"It matters to me," Claire said, staring at his neck, sure she would find a gold chain hanging there. Gil stood on the opposite side of the room, surrounded by women, his view of her blocked. Claire realized she was going to have to handle this situation herself.

"Look, Brad, there are a lot of women here."

"None of them are in our league."

"Well, I'm just not interested."

"C'mon, gimme a chance. To know me is to love me." He did something with his mouth she supposed was meant to be cute. To her, it looked as if he had false teeth and they were slipping.

"Besides," he said, "I've had them already."

"What?" She didn't know whether to laugh or be insulted on behalf of her entire sex.

"They all come here hungry for it," he said, "so I give it to them."

"It?"

"You know what I'm talking about."

"So you don't have a gambling problem?"

"Oh, sure," he said, "I gamble a little, but I don't get carried away."

"So you only come here to…meet people?"

He winked. "You got it, babe."

"I had a couple of friends who used to attend meetings," Claire said.

"What were their names? Maybe I did…ah…knew them."

Claire was going to have to watch this guy carefully. If he recognized the names she gave him as two dead women, he might not talk to her.

"One was Susie Kennedy," Claire said slowly. "She had blond hair—almost white, full-figured, maybe even a little plump, in her early forties."

"Don't know her," Brad said. "I would have noticed her, because she sounds like my type. Who was the other one?"

"Oh, her name was Kathleen Sands."

He frowned. "Hmm, Kathleen Sands. What did she look like?"

"Kind of pretty, dark hair, in her late thirties."

"You know," Brad said, "I think I did see her here— well, not here, but at one of the other locations."

"And did she succumb to your charms?" Clai hoped her sarcasm didn't chase the man away. But he never even noticed.

"That one?" He shook his head. "She was like you, resisting the irresistible. She was more interested in gambling."

"But I thought she came here to break the habit."

"I don't know why she came here, but it sure didn't stop her from doing what she pleased."

"I see."

"But enough about other people," Brad Trager said, "let's talk about us."

She stared at him, exasperated.

TWENTY-NINE

GIL WAS SURROUNDED by four women, all frantically bombarding him with questions and offers of help.

"You can't do this sort of thing alone, you know," one woman said. "You need a sponsor, someone you could call when the urge strikes."

"Yes," another woman agreed, "when that urge strikes, you need to do something to…distract yourself."

Gil thought about telling them he was married and that Claire was there, but maybe he might get more out of them this way.

"I heard about that," he said, "sponsorship, I mean. I had a friend who used to come here, a woman who really needed help."

"What was her name?" a third woman asked. "We're a close-knit group. I probably know her."

"Yes," the second woman said with a smirk, "we know all about one another."

"Is that meant for me, Rita dear?" the third woman asked. "Because if it is—"

"Her name was Kathleen Sands," Gil said. He decided to concentrate on that particular victim because she was the one they knew the least about.

"That bitch!" Rita said.

Gil looked at Rita. She appeared to be the youngest of the four, clearly the most vivacious. She was a tall woman and well proportioned for her height. Her ruffled blouse revealed pale cleavage, and bracelets adorning both arms clanked when she drank her coffee. Her dark hair was teased up too high; she wore a lot of makeup. In fact, he could see the line just below her chin where the makeup ended and her own flesh tone picked up.

The other three women could have been librarians or teachers, the way they dressed, but Rita looked like she could be a cocktail waitress and attract a lot of male attention—in a dark bar, during happy hour.

"You knew her?" Gil asked, trying not to seem too anxious.

"Sure," Rita said, "she came to the meetings acting like she was Miss Diva. You girls remember her. Dark hair, overweight, looked down her nose at the rest of us?"

"That sounds like someone else we know," the third woman muttered. Gil didn't think Rita heard the remark.

"I remember her," the first woman said. "I thought she was nice, but I don't know why she bothered coming here."

"Why do you say that?" Gil asked.

"She was still gambling."

"Right," Rita said over the clank of her bracelets, "not like the rest of us."

The first woman looked hurt. "I haven't been near a Keno machine in months."

"I know you haven't, Francine," the fourth woman said, trying to comfort her.

"Francine," Gil said, "when was the last time you saw Kathleen? I've lost track of her." He got the feeling she had known Kathleen better than the rest.

"You poor man," Francine said.

"What do you mean?"

"She means you ain't gonna see your friend no more," Rita said, slurring her words a bit. Gil wondered if she was adding a little something extra to her coffee. "She went and got herself killed."

"What?"

"Don't you read the papers?"

He opened his brown eyes a bit wider. Whenever Claire accused him of intentionally using that puppy-dog look to get his way, he always denied that he even knew what she was talking about. But he had lied. "Not really."

The women were only too glad to fill Gil in on the gossip, and he listened patiently, as if hearing it all for the first time.

"Three women?" he asked when they were done.

"That's right."

"Did either of the other two women ever come here?"

"Why would you ask that?" Rita wanted to know.

"Just curious."

"I didn't notice them," Francine said, "and I've been to every meeting the past few months, at every location."

"I see."

"Hey, handsome," Rita said, putting her index finger on his chest, "weren't we talking about you needing a sponsor?"

"Well," Gil said, "to tell the truth, I already have one."

"Oh? Who?"

Gil pointed to Claire. "That lady over there, with the Disco King. That's my wife."

"Your wife?" Rita snapped. "You're married?"

He held up his hand so they could see his ring and wiggled his finger.

"Happily," he said. "Well, it's been very nice talking with you ladies, but I'll have to excuse myself; it looks as if my wife needs rescuing."

"He's got some damn nerve bein' married," he heard Rita complain as he walked away.

"EVERYTHING ALL RIGHT, hon?" Gil asked Claire as he came up next to her and put his arm around her waist.

"Whoa, the husband!" Brad said, holding his hand up in a defensive posture. "We were just talkin' here, just talkin'."

"Yes," Claire said, "we were talking about Kathleen Sands."

"Is that so? So was I."

"With those women?" Brad asked. "They didn't treat your friend very well, especially Rita. She didn't like having somebody better-looking around. Fact is, she probably don't like your wife much, and probably ain't never even met her. Am I right or am I right?"

"Well, you're right that we've never been introduced," Claire said.

"After having met Rita," Gil said, "I think he may be right about the first part, too."

"Sure I'm right," Brad said, smiling. "I'm usually right about women."

"Is that so?" Gil asked. "You wouldn't happen to know where Kathleen lived, would you?"

"Naw. Wish I did, though. That would mean I went home with her, ya know? Am I right?"

"When you're right," Gil said, "you're right."

"I need a refill on my coffee," Brad said. "It was nice talking to you, Mrs., uh…"

"Claire," Gil said.

"Right, Claire," Brad said, "nice talkin' to ya."

"Did I interrupt something?" Gil asked as Brad walked away.

"If you hadn't been surrounded by your fan club," Claire said, "you would have noticed a long time ago that I needed help."

"My fan club was telling me about Kathleen Sands."

"And what about the lady with her finger on your chest?"

"You saw that, huh?"

"I did."

"That was Rita."

"Ah, the one who probably doesn't like me. She's a little overdressed for this, don't you think? Or should I say underdressed, the way her boobs are hanging out?"

"What about Brad's chest hair?"

"I wonder why those two aren't together?" Claire asked.

"They probably don't like each other as much as they like themselves."

"Speak of the devil," Claire said. "She's glaring at you right now. What did you do to her?"

"Told her I was married."

Rita was across the room, staring daggers at Gil and talking animatedly to Carlos Delgado. He was listening intently but every now and then would look over at Gil and Claire.

"What do you think she's telling him?" Claire asked.

"I don't know, but we're about to find out. Here he comes."

JUDY BELMONT STOOD apart from the crowd the whole time but watched as Claire and the man she was with got acquainted with the others. Judy knew that Brad Trager was probably hitting on Claire. He had hit on most of the women in the group, except for her and one or two others.

She surmised after awhile that the man was Claire's husband. They made a rather nice-looking couple. He had a full beard and wavy hair. His glasses did make him look a little bookish, but not unattractive. Claire Hunt had it all—a successful television career, a nice husband, probably a beautiful house. Judy wondered how much of the money she spent with the *Home Mall* show had helped pay for Claire's house, and her clothes.

As usual, nobody wanted to talk to Judy. She had never fit into this group, but she kept coming to the meetings only because Whitey insisted. She would rather have been with the women in her shopping club. She looked at her watch and decided she'd been there long enough. Time to go home and tell the exciting news to Whitey. She had seen Claire Hunt in person!

THIRTY

"IMAGINE GETTING kicked out of a Gamblers Anonymous meeting!" Claire said, opening the car door to get in.

"And what about my problem? Who's going to help me now?"

"Oh, we got trouble; we got trouble in River City. And that starts with *t* and rhymes with *p,* which stands for *pool.*"

"Enough with the show tunes," Gil said as he got into the car. "Slot machines—remember, I'm addicted to the slots. I thought I was pretty convincing."

"Can I ask a question?"

"Sure."

"Why aren't you starting the car?"

Gil sat hunched over the wheel, keeping his eyes on the stairway alongside the church. It was getting dark and he didn't want to miss the person he was waiting for.

"One of those women knew more than she let on."

"Which one?" she asked.

"Her name was Francine."

"Which one was she?"

"One of the three with Rita, sniffing out a single man's blood."

"You took your sweet time telling them you were married."

"They probably wouldn't have bothered with me at all if they knew I was spoken for."

"Well, what does she look like? Was she pretty?"

"She looks like my aunt Virginia must have looked at her age."

"I never knew your aunt Virginia."

"Well," Gil said, "let's just say I don't think your friend Brad tried to add her to his list of conquests."

"Conquests," Claire repeated, shaking her head.

"There she is!" He opened the car door and prepared to run after the woman.

"You're going to scare her," Claire said, opening her door. "Let me do it."

"Okay, but hurry."

He watched Claire approach the woman.

"Francine?" Claire called.

"Oh my," Francine said, putting her hand to her chest, "you startled me."

"I'm sorry. I didn't mean to. My name is Claire Hunt. You were talking to my husband earlier, Gil?"

"Oh, yes," Francine said, "I'm afraid we attacked him, didn't we? He is a very nice man, though."

"Yes, he is," Claire agreed.

"You're not mad, are you?" Francine asked, looking suddenly concerned. "You're not going to hit me or anything?"

"Of course not, don't be silly. Gil and I just wanted to talk to you about Kathleen Sands."

"That poor woman. I'm sorry, but I was under the impression—wasn't she a friend of yours, or your husband's?"

"Not really."

"Then I don't understand."

"Could we buy you some coffee and explain?"

"I'm afraid I've had enough coffee for one night."

"Something to eat, then?"

"You know, a hot fudge sundae would be nice," Francine said. "How about Steak 'n Shake?"

"That sounds great."

THIRTY-ONE

THEY DROVE TO the nearest Steak 'n Shake, which was on Lindbergh Boulevard. They parked side by side, since the lot was empty. It was after dinner and before the date crowd hit, so they easily found a table. The black-and-white-tiled floor and chrome fixtures evoked memories of a fifties diner. Claire and Francine both ordered hot fudge sundaes, while Gil opted for one of Steak 'n Shake's famous strawberry shakes.

"I'm sorry, Mr. Hunt, but I thought you told me you knew Kathleen Sands."

"I'm afraid I lied, Francine," Gil said, "and since I wasn't totally honest with you, I think that entitles you to call me Gil." He smiled apologetically.

"All right, Gil," she said, "but if we're going to start over, I also think I deserve an explanation—along with my ice cream—don't you?"

"You certainly do," Gil said, and looked at Claire.

"You go ahead," Claire said, trusting her husband to tell as little or as much as he saw fit.

"I *knew* you looked familiar," Francine said excitedly when Gil got to the part about Claire working for *Home Mall.* "I've seen you on TV."

"Have you bought anything?"

"Oh, no, I just watch…you know, window-shopping, sort of. It's fun."

Gil went on with his explanation and Francine listened intently, hanging on every word. By the time he was done, they had their desserts and were digging into them.

"I understand everything now," Francine said. "This must be very hard on both of you."

"It is," Gil said.

"What can I do to help?" she asked, her tone betraying the fact that she was puzzled.

"We'd like to know where Kathleen Sands lived. We've looked in the phone book, and apparently she's not listed, or she didn't live in St. Louis."

"Oh, she lived in St. Louis; I know that much."

Gil was hoping she'd know more.

"Couldn't you ask the police to give you her address?"

"We tried that," Gil said.

He had bitten the bullet that morning and called Detective Holliday.

"What can I do for you, Mr. Hunt?" Holliday had asked. Gil thought, Uh-oh, last time we saw each other, it was Gil and Jason. Now we're back to Mr. Hunt.

"Well, I was hoping we'd be able to, uh, smooth over the meeting your partner and my wife had yesterday. I understand it didn't go very well."

"That's putting it mildly," Holliday said. "I've got a pretty angry woman on my hands, Mr. Hunt."

"Well, so do I, Detective, but I was hoping cooler heads would prevail."

"Meaning ours?"

"Hopefully."

"Mmmm, why do I think you're leading up to asking me for something?"

"Just an address."

"Can't do it."

"You didn't even ask—"

"You want the address of one of the victims," Holliday said, "probably the Sands woman."

Gil remained silent.

"Am I right?"

"You are."

"See? Can't do it, not with the mood my partner is in now. Besides, you shouldn't be meddling, should you?"

"I'm not meddling."

"Well, I don't think I can help you today, Mr. Hunt. Do you understand?"

"Sure," Gil said, "I understand." But it was only after he'd hung up that he realized Holliday had said "today." If the detective was going to help him, how would he know when?

NOW CLAIRE WAS making a dent in her hot fudge sundae, but not attacking it with the same gusto as the other woman. "The police won't give us her address. They don't want us…asking questions."

"Why not?"

"They say they don't want amateurs meddling in their investigation," Gil said.

"Haven't they ever heard of *Hart to Hart?*"

"I'm sorry?" Claire stopped eating.

"The TV show, *Hart to Hart?* Jonathan and Jennifer? That's who you two remind me of. I think it's wonderful. You guys could be *Hunt to Hunt.*"

"Well…thanks," Claire said. "We think we're pretty wonderful together."

"That's why I'm trying to keep her out of jail, Francine," Gil said.

She put down her spoon then and stared at them with big cow eyes. "That's so romantic."

"And maybe you could help me do it," Gil said. "Do you know where Kathleen Sands lived?"

Francine stared at both of them a moment longer, then picked up her purse, opened it, and took out a small address book.

"We exchanged addresses and phone numbers her first night. I was the only one who would give her the time of day."

"Why was that?" Claire asked.

"Because of Rita," Francine said. "She just thinks she's the beauty queen of GA. As soon as Kathleen walked in, Rita took an instant dislike to her and got all the others to go along."

"What a shame."

"It was," Francine agreed. "Kathleen was nice, but she just didn't really know how to make friends. There's only one other woman in the group like that."

"Who?" Claire asked.

"Judy Belmont."

"Did we meet her?" Gil asked.

"I doubt it. She was standing in a corner all by herself. I don't think she gets along with anyone outside of her shopping group."

Gil and Claire exchanged a glance and then Gil repeated, "Shopping group?"

THIRTY-TWO

As soon as Judy Belmont entered the house, she knew something was wrong. She could feel tension in the air, and Whitey was just sitting on the sofa, as if he'd been staring at the door, waiting for her to come home. In front of him, scattered across the coffee table, were envelopes and papers. Quickly, she recognized them as credit-card bills.

"Whitey—"

"The mail came late today," he said, "so you couldn't hide these from me."

"I can explain."

"Explain what? That you've been spending money faster than I can earn it?"

He snatched up the credit-card bills and held them in his fist. Standing up, he shook them in her face. She flinched. Although he'd never struck her before, she expected him to now.

"They're all from that TV shopping show! Look at these. *Home Mall:* forty-seven fifty. *Home Mall:* fifty-five ninety-five. *Home Mall:* ninety-eight eighty-nine."

Judy wrung her hands. "I'm always careful to stay under a hundred dollars," she said weakly.

"An item? What about the total? What about two thousand dollars *total,* Judy?" A vein stood out like a purple scar on his neck.

"Well...they were things we needed."

"Who told you we need all this stuff?"

"Claire Hunt, from the *Home Mall.*"

"I knew it," he growled.

"And you'll never believe it, Whitey, but she was at the meeting tonight."

She was surprised by his reaction. Suddenly, he calmed down and seemed to forget the bills.

"What?"

"I was surprised, too," Judy said. "I was close enough to touch her, Whitey, but I didn't. I mean, she's from TV—a famous celebrity. I couldn't just walk up and touch her."

"What was she doing at your Gamblers Anonymous meeting?"

"I don't know," Judy said, "but her husband was with her. I think he has the problem, not her. She's much too smart to get hooked on gambling."

"Smarter than you, you mean?"

She put on that hurt look of hers. "Well, I'm sure she's smarter than I am, but I haven't gambled in months, Whitey, you know that."

"Sure I do. But you've replaced gambling with this TV shopping thing! Judy, this is just as bad as when you used to sneak off to the boats."

"No it's not!" she snapped back. "That was gambling, and you said I couldn't gamble anymore, and I haven't!"

He opened his mouth to reply, but she stormed past him into the bathroom and slammed the door. He could hear her crying all the way down the hall. Dropping the bills onto the coffee table, he didn't notice when some of them slid to the floor. The TV was off, thank God.

Judy always had it blaring, when she wasn't off at the mall with her friends, that is.

Claire...what were she and her husband doing at a GA meeting? This bothered Whitey. It was bad enough that this Claire was always talking Judy into buying things. What if she showed up at the next meeting and Judy started talking to her? What could this woman convince her to do if she actually talked to her—face-to-face?

Whitey walked into the kitchen and looked at the calendar, where they had all of Judy's meetings written down. The next scheduled one was in five days.

That gave him less than a week to decide what to do.

THIRTY-THREE

GIL WAS THE FIRST ONE out of bed the next morning. He wanted to talk to Claire before she left for work, and he thought breakfast would be the perfect time.

"You *made* me eat that hot fudge sundae last night," Claire playfully complained over her tea. "Now I'll have to watch what I eat all day." She bit into an English muffin slathered with peanut butter.

"*I* made you eat it?"

"Whose idea was it to go to Steak 'n Shake anyway?"

"I think it was Francine's," he said around a mouthful of muffin covered with butter and jelly.

"Yes, well…what did you think of everything she said, now that you've slept on it?"

"She certainly knows everyone's business over there." Gil said. "And thank goodness she does, because now we've got Kathleen Sands's address and can check it out today."

"More relatives," she said, shaking her head. "I still haven't recovered from talking to Mary Dunn's sister."

"Well, I guess you're excused, since you have to go into the station—but only if you have a note from your mother."

Claire reached across the table and smoothed a piece

of Gil's hair down around his ear. "Did I ever tell you it's your sense of humor that makes you so sexy?"

He kissed her hand. "What about my abnormally large muscles? And my handsome, rugged looks?"

She laughed. "See what I mean? You're so funny!"

He faked a hurt look.

"But seriously," Claire said, "maybe we should go together."

"We can meet afterward and I'll fill you in. Meanwhile, let's talk about this Judy Belmont and her shopping group."

"Could it be the same group Buxton told you about? What did he call them? Oh, yeah, the Shopping Fools."

"Well, if it's not the same, it's one hell of a coincidence."

"What do we do about it?"

"That's simple," Gil said. "We'll have to talk to Judy Belmont."

"How do we find her?"

"We'll try the usual methods first."

"Usual methods?" She grinned. "We're starting to develop usual methods? You make us sound so professional."

"We're a couple of detectives, we are," Gil said.

"You heard Francine. We're *Hunt to Hunt*."

"I liked that, didn't you?" Gil asked.

"It was kind of cute. What if the usual method, meaning the phone book, is as little help as it was with Kathleen Sands?"

"Then we might have to use the same method we used last night."

"Go to another meeting?"

"Francine said the next one's in five days."

"Where is it this time?"

"Some church on Olive called the Congregation of His Almighty Power."

"These churches have great names, don't they?" Claire commented. "I wonder if they're all divinely inspired?"

He licked jelly off his fingers. "Somebody gets paid to do it, I bet. Why I even bet there's an eight hundred number you call. Hello? I want to start up a church and I need a name—a catchy name. Church of the Casino Queen? Thank you. I'll mail you my fifty bucks today."

She rolled her eyes. "Gil, we can't go to another meeting; we got kicked out last night, remember? After Rita told Mr. Delgado about all the questions we were asking, he got upset."

"We weren't really kicked out," Gil said. We were asked—very politely—to leave."

"And asked never to come back."

"We don't have to attend the meeting, Claire. We'll just wait outside for her to come out and then we'll approach her like we did Francine."

"She didn't strike me as the talkative type."

Gil sat up a little straighter. "You spoke to her?"

"No," Claire said, "but after Francine described her, I thought I remembered seeing her. There was a woman in the corner and she was just…well, staring."

"At what?"

"At me."

"Maybe she recognized you."

"Maybe, but it made me very uncomfortable."

"Well, you can tell her that when we meet her," Gil said.

"That's five days from now. What do we do until then?"

"We try to find relatives belonging to Kathleen Sands and Susie Kennedy."

"But we've already tried to find Susie Kennedy's people and we keep coming up empty."

"So, we'll try again."

She shook her head, stood up, and tightened the sash at the waist of her terry-cloth robe. "I wish I had your patience," she said. Then she began gathering up their cups and plates.

He came up behind her and put his arms around her waist as she stood in front of the kitchen sink. "You have me," he said into her ear, "and I have enough patience for both of us."

She leaned back against him and they stood that way for a little while before getting dressed and venturing out into the world.

THIRTY-FOUR

THE ADDRESS Francine gave Gil and Claire turned out to be an old schoolhouse that had been renovated and divided into apartments. It was located in Soulard, a neighborhood originally settled by many Eastern European groups, especially the Czechs. The Soulard market, famous for its fruits, vegetables, and flowers, had been in operation for more than 150 years. The area was still charming, with its redbrick row houses, but constantly being rehabed and refurbished by urban homesteaders.

Gil mounted the steps and examined mailboxes outside the large front door. Francine wasn't sure which apartment Kathleen Sands had occupied, but there it was plain as day: KATHLEEN SANDS, 2D.

Gil pressed the bell, waited a few minutes, then pressed it again. When he still received no answer, he pushed the bells for 1A, 1B, 2A, 2B, and a few others. Obviously, the people who lived there went to work during the day. This was going to be a big bust if he couldn't even get into the building.

He pressed a few more bells and finally someone answered.

"Yes?"

"Uh..." He wasn't sure which apartment he had disturbed. "I'm sorry...I'm looking for Kathleen Sands."

"Apartment two D," the voice said. He thought it was a woman, although it sounded distorted.

"Uh, wait—I pressed it and no one answered."

There was a long moment of silence and then the voice said, "Oh, that's right. She's dead. You did hear that she died, didn't you? I mean, you're not a relative and I just told you that over the intercom?"

"No, I'm not a relative, and yes, I knew she died. Could I ask you some questions about her?"

"Are you a reporter?"

"No."

"Then who are you?"

"This would be easier face-to-face."

"I'm not letting you in if you don't tell me who you are. In fact, I think I'll call the police right now."

"That's a good idea," Gil said. "Call the Major Case Squad and ask for Detective Holliday. He'll vouch for me."

"I need to know your name before I can ask him."

"Gil Hunt."

"And?"

"And I own a bookstore, but this isn't getting us anywhere. Look, some other women have been murdered the same way Kathleen was, and I'm trying to help find out who did it."

"Make up your mind. Are you a bookstore owner or a detective?"

"I'm not any kind of detective," he said, "I'm just a guy who's trying to help his wife."

Nothing happened for a few moments and then the voice said, "Come on up. I'm in two F." Seconds later, she buzzed the door open and Gil went in.

He walked up to the second floor and found the woman standing in the brightly painted hall in front of her apartment. She had red hair trimmed neatly in a bob. Her complexion was pale and freckled. She had an artsy way about her that Gil thought was very attractive. She was wearing a smock spattered with flecks of various colors. She was obviously in the middle of painting something, and Gil wondered if it was a canvas or her apartment.

As he reached her, Gil realized he hadn't paid any attention to her name on the mailbox. In the next moment, she bailed him out.

"My name is Maureen Concannon. I'd offer to shake hands, but mine are covered with paint. No, I'm not painting my apartment; I'm an artist."

And a psychic, Gil thought.

"Just out of curiosity, why did you let me in?"

"You mentioned Detective Holliday. He interviewed me...about Kathleen. And I am kind of psychic. I could sense you were troubled, not trouble."

"You're right," he said, "I am troubled. Can we talk inside?"

"We can talk out here," she said, "for two reasons. One, I'm working on something and I don't let anyone see my work in progress."

"Okay."

"And two, I may be intuitive, but I'm not stupid. I don't just let strangers into my home."

"It seems to me you're in as much danger out here as you'd be in there."

She took her hand out from behind her back and showed him what looked like an electric razor. "Stun gun," she said. "Besides, what if you just wanted to see the inside of my apartment to check if I had anything worth stealing? No, we can talk out here, Mr. Hunt."

"Fine with me."

"Now, tell me how I can help you."

Gil tried to get comfortable by leaning against the wall. "Let's start with how well you knew Kathleen Sands."

"We weren't friends, if that's what you mean. We'd pass in the hall, say hello, talk about the weather. I found her pleasant. She had a good aura. So how well did you know her, Mr. Hunt?"

He explained about Claire—who she was, what she did, and the pressure she was under.

"You love your wife very much," Maureen Concannon said when he was finished. "I can certainly feel that."

"Yes, I do."

"There's something I don't understand, however."

"What's that?"

"Why do the police suspect your wife just because there was a tape of her at each scene? That doesn't make sense to me."

"It doesn't make sense to me, either."

"No, I mean it's not logical. I spoke with Detective Holliday and his partner. Neither seemed stupid, although she did have a fairly dark aura."

"What would that indicate?"

"It could mean a lot of things. That she's ill, she's heading for trouble, or she's simply a very negative person."

"I'd vote for the last one."

"But are those tapes enough of a reason to suspect your wife of murder?"

Gil frowned. "No, but they do tie her to each murder scene. And since we haven't received any threats against her life, she's not in danger. Which, as far as the police are concerned, leaves Claire free to commit murder, I guess.''

Maureen shook her head. ''I'm sorry, but I don't think I can be of any more help to you today, Mr. Hunt, and I do have a canvas waiting for me.''

''Just a few more minutes, please,'' he said. ''Can't you think of anything else? Something that might help me?''

Maureen hesitated a moment. ''She was quiet, clean, pleasant—but I said that before. I guess I could tell you where she worked.''

''You could? That would be a great help.''

''She was a hostess in a restaurant over on Olive. What was the name of that place? Oh, damn, it's on the tip of my tongue.'' She struggled with the memory a few more minutes. ''Oh shit! This is annoying.''

''Maybe you have it written down somewhere? I could wait out here while—''

''No, no,'' she said, ''I didn't write it down. Why would I? She just happened to mention it one day. I'll remember it, though…. Can I call you? I'm sure it'll be tonight. I'll remember it while I'm working. That's what always happens.''

''All right.'' Gil didn't carry business cards, but he did have bookmarks that he'd had made up some time ago, and he usually carried a few with him. This time, he had just one, and he found it folded inside his pocket. It had the name, address, and phone number of the store printed in raised black letters.

''I'll write my home number here, too.''

She accepted the bookmark and looked at it. ''Do you carry art books?''

''Some. I have a little bit of everything.''

''New Age?''

"I do have a New Age section, as a matter of fact."

"I'll have to drop by."

"Please do. I'll give you a nice discount for your help."

She put her hand on the doorknob. "And as soon as I remember the name of the restaurant, I'll give you a call."

"Thanks so much."

"I hope it helps." She opened the door just wide enough to slide inside.

Gil went back downstairs and out the front door, all the while rehashing what Maureen had said. He blamed fear, the shock of being included in a murder investigation—all of it—for pulling him and Claire in too close to think clearly. Talk about not seeing the forest for the trees. It had taken an unbiased stranger to make Gil fully understand how unfair the investigating officers had been treating him and his wife.

The more he thought about it, the angrier he got. Before he could talk himself out of it, he decided to go directly to Detective Holliday's office while he was still mad enough to speak his mind.

THIRTY-FIVE

GIL HUNT HAD a notoriously long fuse, but the more time he had to think about what Claire had been going through, the shorter it got. When he finally arrived at Holliday's office at the Major Case Squad, he was furious and demanded to see the detective. He was immediately shown into the squad room.

Holliday was there, seated behind his desk, dressed in a short-sleeved shirt, looking harried. Although there were other people in the room, Myra Longfellow was nowhere in sight. Holliday looked up as Gil approached, having been warned of Gil's arrival in advance by the front desk.

"I've got to talk to you," Gil began, his heart pounding the way it did whenever he got worked up. His voice shook. He *hated* getting this way; that's why it always took so long. He also felt stupid that he hadn't done this before, damn it; this was about *Claire!*

"Sit down, Mr. Hunt."

"I don't want to sit down!" Gil snapped. "I think my wife has gone through enough of this bullshit, Holliday. There's no earthly reason she should have to suffer the pressure of being a suspect when there's no goddamned evidence—"

"You're right."

"—that she was even... What?"

Holliday stood up and leaned across his desk. Gil could smell the perspiration coming off the man's body.

"I said you're right, Mr. Hunt, but I'm not going to discuss anything with you if you're going to stand there shouting like a maniac. Either sit down or I'll kick your ass out of here."

Gil was taken aback momentarily. When he sat down, Holliday did the same.

"I'm right?"

"Yes, sir. We have no evidence against Mrs. Hunt."

"The tapes…"

"The tapes draw your wife into the equation, certainly, but they're not reason enough to suspect her."

"But you said—"

"I don't think I ever said she was a suspect."

"Well, your partner sure as hell did," Gil said. "In fact, she said it when they met right here."

"I know, but my partner has very different thoughts on this case than I do. The fact of the matter is, if she suspects your wife, it's based more on intuition than any hard evidence."

Gil sat back in his chair and studied Holliday for a moment.

"Why are you telling me this?"

"Because from what I can see, your wife's a real nice lady. Don't get me wrong. If she did it and I could prove it, I'd lock her up. I just don't happen to think she's guilty."

"Well," Gil said, "she'll be glad to hear that. What about your partner?"

"My partner doesn't like your wife and there's nothing I can do about that."

"Which is about as illogical to me as suspecting her of anything."

Holliday smiled. "Sure, you'd say that. You're her husband. You can't think of any reason why anyone would dislike her."

"You're right. I can't." Gil leaned forward. "What about helping us with—"

"No can do. Your wife brought in information we already had. I have to warn you again not to interfere with a police investigation."

Gil decided not to tell Holliday he had just come from Kathleen Sands's building. They were on official ground, and Holliday seemed to be conducting himself accordingly—except for telling Gil that Claire wasn't a suspect in his opinion.

"Go home, Mr. Hunt," Holliday said. "Put your wife's mind at ease."

The use of Gil's last name confirmed what he had been thinking: that being on a first name basis when having lunch together at Fitz's was one thing, but this was entirely another.

"I'd like to, Detective. However, I need to know one more thing."

Holliday waited.

"Do you think my wife is a potential victim?"

"I won't lie to you," Holliday said. "Somebody obviously wants her dragged into this, but I haven't the faintest idea why. Is she next in line to be murdered? I don't know, but if I were you, I'd keep a close eye on her."

Gil studied the man again. Clearly, he wasn't going to offer anything more. Not here in a room surrounded by other detectives.

"Okay," he said, standing up. "All right…. I'm sorry about bursting in here."

"Forget it."

Gil nodded. Neither man seemed very comfortable at the moment. Gil decided that any further discussion in this environment was useless. Maybe later he could get Holliday on neutral turf.

"Well...thanks," Gil said.

"Have a good day, Mr. Hunt."

Gil turned to walk out of the squad room, but when he got to the door, Detective Longfellow appeared. They stared at each other for a few moments before she grudgingly moved aside to let him pass.

"What the hell did he want?" Longfellow asked Holliday.

"He's just worried about his wife."

"Well, he should be. She's hiding something."

"Give it a rest, Myra," Holliday said wearily.

"What?"

"The poor woman is probably in danger of being killed herself, not a killer."

Longfellow put her hands on her hips and glared at him. "Did you tell him she wasn't a suspect?"

"I told him that as far as I was concerned, she wasn't. I can't speak for you."

"You could back me on this, Jason," Longfellow said accusingly.

"How, Myra? There's no evidence against Mrs. Hunt. What do you have against her, anyway?"

"Nothing. Why should I? I'm just doing my job."

"Fine," Holliday said, "let's both do our jobs and keep personal feelings out of it."

"Better take your own advice."

"What's that supposed to mean?"

"It means I think you've got a thing for Mrs. Hunt, that's what."

"You know, Myra," Holliday said, "if you were a man…"

"Yeah? If I was a man, what?"

Holliday looked up at her and said, "You'd be a real prick."

THIRTY-SIX

"YOU DID *WHAT?*" Claire asked over dinner. He had called her at the studio and asked her to meet him at Café Napoli, not far from their condo.

"Well," he amended, "I *started* to tear into him, but he stopped me."

"How?"

"By agreeing with me."

"Wait," she said, putting down her fork, ignoring her pasta. "Start from the beginning."

He did, telling her about Maureen Concannon and then about going to Holliday's office to confront him.

"Why did you decide to do this now?" Claire asked.

Gil shrugged. "I don't know, but I sure as hell should have done it long before now. There was never any reason for you to be a suspect, and it shouldn't have taken a conversation with a psychic artist to push me into questioning it."

"You're so sweet," Claire said, reaching over and taking his hand. "What else did this psychic artist tell you?"

"She said I was very much in love with my wife and that it showed."

"Is that true?"

"Would I lie?"

"No, I know you love me," Claire said, "I meant, is it true that she said those exact words?"

"Of course."

"Hmm," she said, withdrawing her hand and reclaiming her fork again. "I'd like to meet this woman."

"Once you get past the stun gun, she's very nice."

Claire laughed. "I'm liking her more and more. So Holliday agreed that I'm not a suspect?"

"Well, not as far as he's concerned."

"But to his partner, I am."

"He doesn't know what her problem is," Gil said, finally paying attention to his dinner, "but they don't agree on you, that's for sure."

"Well, I don't want to come between them—but good. I don't like that woman, Gil."

"And the feeling is definitely mutual."

"I only wish I knew what's behind her horrible attitude toward me."

"Well," Gil said, "it should ease your mind just knowing that Holliday doesn't suspect you."

"If not me, then who?"

"He candidly admitted they have no suspects."

"That doesn't put my mind at ease at all," she said. "Some crazy person is still out there, and they apparently have a collection of tapes with me on them."

"Don't worry, honey, we're going to keep looking." Gil knew how lame his statement sounded, but he hoped Claire hadn't noticed.

"Looking for what?"

"Answers."

"Gil," she said, putting her fork down again, "are we looking for the killer? And if so, what are we supposed to do if we find him? We're not the police."

"We're just trying to get some answers, Claire. Something we can give to Holliday that he can't ignore. Believe me, I don't like it any more than you do that some nut is out there who apparently wants to involve you in this.''

Claire frowned and picked up her wineglass. ''I wonder who it is. I think about it every day. Who knows me, and wants to harm me-and will that person suddenly decide to hurt me physically?''

''Well,'' Gil said, ''I'm not about to let *that* happen.''

''I love you,'' she said, ''but how effective would either of us be against a killer?''

''Claire,'' he said, taking her hand now, ''I will never let anyone hurt you.''

''I know, but I really think we should leave this to the police now.''

''But we have a couple of great leads. We have to go to the next GA meeting. And Maureen is going to call us with the name of the restaurant where Kathleen Sands worked. What's the harm in seeing what develops?''

''You know what, Gilbert Hunt?''

He winced. ''What?''

''I think you're starting to enjoy playing detective.''

''I think you better start enjoying your dinner,'' Gil countered, ''before it gets cold.''

WHEN THEY RETURNED home, the light was blinking on their answering machine, indicating one message. Gil pressed the button.

''Mr. Hunt? This is Maureen Concannon. I remembered the name of Kathleen's restaurant. It was called the King's Room and it's out on Lindbergh somewhere, uh, North Lindbergh. I'm sure you can get the address from them, or the phone book. I hope this helps you…oh, and your wife. I still intend to drop by your store sometime. Guess I'll see you then. Bye.''

"'Oh, and your wife,'" Claire repeated breathily. "'I still intend to drop by your store…see you then… Bye.' That was your psychic artist, huh?''

"That was her," Gil said. "She came through with that restaurant. We can check it out tomorrow.''

"And you can bet I'll be in your store when this psychic friend drops in, so I can check *her* out.''

"Don't be silly.''

"She wants you," Claire said, "I could hear it in her voice. You know, I'm a little psychic myself, Mr. Hunt.''

"Really?'' He reached out and pulled her to him. "What am I thinking right now?''

She hesitated just a moment, frowning as if she were concentrating on reading his mind. "You're thinking that I look great in my new blouse and I should wear this shade of blue more often.''

"Well, it's true, you do, and you should, but that's not exactly what was on my mind.''

"You're no challenge at all.'' She took his hand and led him to the bedroom. "No challenge at all.''

THIRTY-SEVEN

CLAIRE WOKE UP early the next morning and, letting Gil sleep, fixed herself an easy breakfast of cold cereal. She kissed him good-bye, causing him to stir but not wake, and left for the studio.

IT WAS SEVERAL HOURS later when Gil awoke. He got up and, seeing the cereal box Claire had left on the counter, decided he was hungry. Slicing a banana on top of his cornflakes, he checked the clock. A sales representative from a local small press was meeting him at the store at nine. There was still plenty of time before he had to leave. Allyn Marcus had classes that day, but the young man had promised to come in after four o'clock and hold down the fort until closing. Gil didn't mind, though; in fact, he looked forward to being in the store. He had some serious thinking to do and usually was able to concentrate better surrounded by the books—insulated by them.

WHEN CLAIRE ARRIVED at the studio, she was met by her product coordinator, a pretty young blonde named Kate Pyatt. Kate worked with all the show hosts, but she had a special fondness for Claire and showed it by going the extra mile whenever she could. On this particular day, she greeted Claire with a cup of tea.

"Thanks, Kate. Nice to have you back. Are you done with classes already?"

"I took my last final yesterday. But I couldn't wait to get back; I've heard all about the murders, Claire." Kate's eyes were always so wide with youthful wonder. Claire couldn't remember if she'd been that wide-eyed at twenty. "It's terrible about those tapes." Kate twisted one of the sterling rings on her finger.

"Where did you hear about them?" Claire asked.

"Oh, I've been in touch with some of the guys here." They both walked over to Claire's makeup table. "Who do you suppose has been leaving them?"

"I don't know," Claire said, setting down her tea and picking up a comb. "The police are working on it." She didn't bother to tell the young girl that she and Gil were also.

Kate gasped. "Maybe it's somebody who's jealous of you and wants your job."

"I doubt that," Claire said. "I don't think anyone would be jealous of me."

"But you're on TV, and excellent at what you do."

"Thanks, Kate." Claire wanted to change the subject. "Could you run and get me the list of items we'll be showing this morning?"

"Oh, sure," Kate said, striking her forehead with the heel of her hand. "I've been away so long, I forgot. I'll get it."

Claire was relieved when Kate left. She wanted to work on her makeup and think. Under normal circumstances, she enjoyed the girl's enthusiasm, but this morning it was just too overwhelming.

Claire was worried about Gil. He had gotten so wrapped up in his "investigation." What if the killer noticed him and went after him? What if he—or they—

had already crossed paths with the killer, and he recognized them both now? Could he have been at the GA meeting? Maybe Delgado? Or Disco Brad? What if it was a woman? She shuddered to think she might have actually shaken hands with the person who had strangled three women.

Her thoughts were interrupted when Kate returned. "Here you go. Can I get you some more tea?"

"Thanks, that would be nice." Claire handed Kate the cup and watched as the girl walked away. She always reminded Claire of how she herself had looked all those years ago when her hair had hung long and free and her clothes had been tie-dyed.

Returning her attention to preparing for the morning show, Claire started reading down the list while applying fresh lipstick.

GIL FINISHED his breakfast and got himself another cup of coffee. Before leaving for the store, he liked to tune in to Claire's morning show, just to get a look at her. He was always impressed when he got to watch her doing her job. He wondered if she felt the same. After all, businesses had come and gone in the University City Loop, but he had survived in the same location for years. He might not be a TV personality, but he'd served as president of the University City Merchants' Association, sponsored many book fairs in town, even been asked to run for mayor. But he'd turned down the offer—which was repeated from time to time—because it would take him away from the store. Gil had degrees in American and European literature, was an expert appraiser of first editions. But above and beyond the vital statistics, he truly loved what he did. He had experienced firsthand some of the fuss made over Claire by women who recognized her, and he knew he wouldn't be as comfortable with celebrity as Claire was. No, he was happiest in his store, and going on booking trips with Claire.

He watched Claire now, seated in front of a set decorated to give the illusion of a cozy country kitchen. She was talking about a canister set on the table in front of her. She had been on the air for about an hour.

He had to leave in a few minutes to open the store, and he had only a few sips of coffee left in his cup when he realized something was wrong. Gil usually tuned the callers out, but the look on Claire's face and her demeanor claimed his full attention.

"I—I'm sorry?" Claire said, her eyes darting from side to side as if she wasn't sure what to do. "What did you say?"

The man spoke in a growl. "I said it's your fault they're dead."

Gil sat up straight. Thurman had been too cheap to install any kind of delay system for phone calls so they could weed out the nuts.

"People like psychos," he'd said. "They'll tune in just to hear one."

To date, this hadn't hurt the station any, because apparently nuts didn't usually call into shopping shows.

"Well," Gil said to the TV, "it looks like you've got one on your hands right now, Ben, old buddy."

CLAIRE COULDN'T BELIEVE her ears. She looked at Harve Wilson, who spread his hands, at a loss as to what to do. Cut the guy off! she wanted to shout at him, but the caller spoke again.

"Are you shocked? That I blame you, Claire?"

She was getting angry now. "Yes, I am. Why would you?"

"Because you made me do it," the caller said. "You made me kill them."

Claire felt a chill settle in the pit of her stomach because she knew—she *knew*—this guy was telling the truth. She just wasn't sure what to do about it.

Through his headset, Harve Wilson listened to his boss, Benjamin Thurman.

"Don't you dare cut him off!" Thurman shouted. "This is priceless."

"Boss," Wilson said, "Claire's not gonna—"

"She'll be fine. She'll handle him; she's a pro. Don't do a thing, Harve, or your ass is outta here."

"Okay, okay," Harve Wilson said, and once again he shrugged helplessly at Claire.

SHE WAS HANDLING HERSELF wonderfully well, Gil thought. But when the guy actually said he was the killer, Gil could see by the look on his wife's face that she believed him. He grabbed the phone and dialed Jason Holliday's number. Luckily, the detective was in.

"What?" Holliday asked.

"I said the killer is on TV with Claire right now. Can't you do something?" Gil shouted. "Trace the call!"

"All right, all right, Gil, calm down," Holliday said. "We'll get on it. I'll drive down to the station."

"I'll see you there," Gil said, and hung up on Holliday's protest.

Before leaving, however, he went to the TV for a moment and crouched in front of it. Putting his hand on the glass, as if the gesture would somehow let Claire know he was there, he said, "Hang on, baby." Then he turned the TV off and hurried out the door.

WHEN GIL GOT to the station, there were more cars in the lot than usual. He wouldn't have recognized Holliday's car, but he assumed the detective must have gotten there before he had.

Gil entered the building and quickly made his way to the *Home Mall* studio. Claire was in her chair backstage. Jason Holliday was standing next to her, and Myra Longfellow was off to the side, talking to some of the crew members. Gil marched right up to Claire, who reached out for him with one hand. Gil held it tightly.

"I knew you were watching," she said. "Detective Holliday said you called him."

"Were you able to trace the call?" Gil demanded.

Holliday shook his head. "We didn't have time."

"What? You mean with call waiting, call forwarding, caller ID, and all sorts of computers, you still can't trace a simple phone call?"

"It takes awhile to get a trace going, Gil," Holliday said, "and the caller didn't stay on long enough."

"How long *was* he on?"

"It seemed like forever," Claire said. "Where's Harve? I'm going to kill him."

But she didn't move. In truth, her legs were still too weak for her to stand. She was furious with her director for making her go through the whole ordeal, but she was also a little exhilarated at having been able to talk to the killer.

"Was it really him?" Gil asked.

"That's something we're going to have to try to establish," Holliday said. "Who's the director here?"

"Harve Wilson."

"Myra?"

"I'll get him," Kate Pyatt said. She had been anxiously waiting for something to do.

"Thank you, Miss," Longfellow said, and resumed her conversation.

"What about a producer?" Holliday asked. "I'm really ignorant about what goes on here. Do you have one?"

"Just Ben—Mr. Thurman," Claire said. "He owns the station, and he pretty much produces everything we do."

"Where was he when all of this was going on?"

"Upstairs in his office, I assume. He usually watches the shows from there."

"Here's Harve," Kate said, returning to Claire's side.

"Mr. Wilson," Holliday said, "how do you usually handle nut calls?"

"We disconnect them as soon as we realize they're not, uh, legitimate." Harve wiped the perspiration from his forehead with a soiled handkerchief.

"Would you kindly tell me, then, why you didn't cut this caller off when you realized what was happening?"

"Mr. Thurman wouldn't let me."

"Clai—Mrs. Hunt just told me that Thurman was in his office upstairs."

"That's right," Wilson said, "but he's in direct contact with me through my headset. When he realized what the man was talking about, he immediately ordered me not to disconnect."

"Is there tape on this show?"

"Yes," Wilson said. "We make tapes down here, and Mr. Thurman records everything upstairs."

"Well, then," Holliday said, looking at his partner, "I guess we talk to Mr. Thurman next."

Gil turned toward the detective. "I'm coming with you."

"Me, too," Claire chimed in. She stood, still holding on to Gil's hand.

"Claire," Wilson said helplessly, "I'm sorry, but..."

"It's okay, Harve, I'll take it up with Ben."

As the three walked by camera two, Linda Bennett leaned over and grabbed Claire's sleeve. "I can't believe that son of a bitch did this to you. Nail his ass to the wall!"

Claire smiled at the pretty camerawoman. "Thanks, that's just what I intend to do."

THIRTY-EIGHT

HOLLIDAY PAUSED to stare at the word janitor on the door leading to Benjamin Thurman's office. Thurman stood from behind his desk as Gil, Claire, and the two detectives entered. Before anyone had a chance to speak, Claire walked up to Thurman and slapped his face.

No one moved for a second. Thurman rubbed his reddening cheek and finally said to Claire, "Is this the opening negotiation for a raise?"

"You son of a—"

"I think you'll both have to save this discussion for another time," Holliday interrupted. "Mr. Thurman, I'm Detective Holliday, and this is my partner, Detective Longfellow."

"How do you do," Thurman said, removing his hand from his face to shake Holliday's hand. The red imprint was still there. "Won't you have a seat?"

"I don't have time for that right now, sir," Holliday said. "You've had something very unusual happen here today."

"I'm well aware of that, Detective," Thurman said. "It's not every day I get slapped in the face by an employee." He glared at Claire.

"I was talking about the phone call Mrs. Hunt received while she was on the air."

"Yes," Thurman said happily, "a phone call from a killer. That's a once-in-a-lifetime event."

"We don't know for sure that the man is a killer," Holliday said.

"Claire does," Thurman said. "Don't you, Claire?"

Claire turned away from Thurman and looked at Holliday. "It was him."

"And how on earth do you know that?" Longfellow asked smugly.

"I just do," Claire said. "I felt it—I still feel it."

Holliday gave his partner a disapproving glance as she mumbled her disbelief under her breath. "Mrs. Hunt, you'll forgive us for not being able to take your word for it."

Claire simply looked away. She had little use at that moment for any of the people in the room other than her husband.

"Ben, did you get the call on videotape?" Gil asked.

"Of course; I tape all my programs."

"Well, that's what Detective Holliday is interested in, I'm sure."

"Thank you, Mr. Hunt," Holliday said. "Mr. Thurman, we'd like to view that tape."

"Of course," Thurman said. "It's already loaded into the machine."

There was an elaborate setup against one wall, virtually a home entertainment center gone mad. Thurman picked up his remote control and pressed a button. Claire appeared in the center of the screen, just moments before the call came in. They all settled down to watch.

CLAIRE: You're on the air with Claire.

CALLER: It's your fault, you know?

CLAIRE (*laughing*): I—I'm sorry? What did you say?

CALLER: I said it's your fault they're dead.

CLAIRE: What?

CALLER: Are you shocked? That I blame you, Claire?

CLAIRE: Yes, I am. Why would you?

CALLER: Because you made me do it. You made me kill them.

CLAIRE (*eyes darting about for a moment, then realizing she won't be getting any help*): Are you telling me that you killed those three women?

CALLER: With my own two hands.

CLAIRE: Then why is it my fault?

CALLER (*forcefully*): Because I said it is!

CLAIRE (*calm now*): All right, all right, take it easy.

CALLER: You seduce people.

CLAIRE: What people?

CALLER: The women who watch you. You seduce them into buying things they don't need. You make them spend all their money, money that's been earned by—

CLAIRE: By you? Are you saying those women were spending your money?

CALLER: Of course not! They made their own money, but they made—

CLAIRE: Yes? They made somebody else spend your—

CALLER: That's enough. I just called to tell you that even though I'm onto you, there won't be any more women killed.

CLAIRE: Well, that's a relief.

CALLER: Once you're dead, Claire!

Click!

Everyone in the room watched Claire, whose feet were riveted to the floor by what she had just heard on the TV.

"Wasn't she great?" Thurman asked.

Gil moved closer to his wife. "I hate to agree with him," he said softly, "but you were."

"You did real well, Mrs. Hunt," Holliday said.

The one dissenting vote in the room came from Detective Longfellow. "Not one thing on that tape proves you were actually speaking to the killer."

"I'm afraid my partner's right," Holliday said.

"You weren't able to trace the call," Gil said, "so what's the difference?"

"Actually," Thurman said, "that's not really true."

They all turned and looked at him.

"What do you mean?" Holliday asked.

"I'm not as cheap as most people think I am."

"Meaning?" Claire asked.

"There are three main phone lines coming into the building. Our general ordering number has almost one hundred extensions. But customer service and the management offices have only five phones each."

"Are you saying you monitor all the calls on those

last two lines?'' Holliday asked. ''You're a little bit of a control freak, aren't you?''

Thurman smiled at the detective and said, ''There's no little bit about it.''

''So you were in on the call from the start?'' Longfellow asked. ''How does that help us?''

''That doesn't help us at all,'' Thurman said, ''but this does.'' He pointed to a little white box on his desk.

''What's that?'' Holliday asked.

But Gil knew. ''Benjamin Thurman, you son of a bitch,'' he said, shaking his head. ''You've got caller ID on every line.''

THIRTY-NINE

CLAIRE STRETCHED to reach the shelf. "I don't see why I have to be on this wobbly ladder and you get to sit safely on the floor."

"First of all, it's not a ladder; it's a dinky little step stool. Second, I have to unpack and log in the books before I hand them to you. And third—"

"I know, I know. I asked to come in and help, so I deserve what I get," she said, looking down at him.

"No, I was going to say that I get a better look at your legs from here."

She turned back to the shelf. "Everything in our life is going crazy and you still take time to notice me...or at least joke about it."

"Like I keep telling you, it's my job."

It had been just one day since the incident at TBN. Benjamin Thurman had shown no emotion about putting Claire in such a precarious spot, other than the embarrassment when she'd slapped him. At Holliday's suggestion and Gil's insistence, he ended up giving her a two-week vacation, all expenses paid. Even though viewer response had been overwhelming and kept circuits jammed all day, Thurman hadn't succeeded in business by dumb luck. No, he knew a great thing when he saw—or heard it—and he wanted to keep Claire happy anyway he could. If it made her husband feel more like a man, thinking he was protecting her, so be it. Claire Hunt's predicament was temporary, but her marketability, Thurman knew, was permanent.

"I don't know what I'd do without you," she said.

"Look at it this way, we get to spend more time together. You get to relax and bum around in your jeans and that horrible T-shirt I hate so much."

"Hey! This was a gift from my fan club in Omaha," she said, pulling at the restaurant logo printed beneath a red heifer.

"It's still ugly," he said. "I know! How about if we take a trip? There's that B and B you've been wanting to stay at up in Wisconsin. We could take long walks, stay in bed all day, eat too much…"

"Back up to the bed part."

He handed her another book. "Get your mind out of the gutter, Mrs. Hunt. Right now, we have work to do."

"What a slave driver," she playfully complained. "Talking about slave driver…what do you think I should do about Ben?"

"Isn't that the point of this whole leave of absence? To keep you out of sight awhile and let things cool off between you and Ben? I think he did as much as he could by way of apologizing," Gil said.

"But I don't feel the same toward him now."

"You always said he was a jerk."

"Yeah, but he was a decent jerk, you know? A character," Claire said. "We didn't have to see eye-to-eye to have a good working relationship; I respected him. But now…"

"Now what?"

"I don't trust him and I don't think I like him very much. Maybe I never will."

Gil reached up and rubbed her leg. "You know whatever you decide is okay with me. Besides, I could always fire Allyn and hire you. I'd even give you two dollars above minimum wage."

"My hero."

When the phone suddenly rang, Gil let the machine take the call. Officially, the store wouldn't be open for a few more hours.

"You have reached the Old Delmar Bookstore; we do not open until noon. Please leave a message or call back then. Thank you."

Beep.

"Mr. Hunt? Mrs. Hunt? Are you there? This is Detective Holliday. Gil? If you're there, pick up."

While Gil made a dash for the phone, Claire jumped down to the wooden floor.

"Yes, Detective, I'm here."

"Good. Is Mrs. Hunt with you? I called your condo and got the machine."

"Yes, she's here." He motioned for her to pick up the extension on his desk in the back of the store. "Why? Has something happened?"

"Well, we traced the number of the caller on Mr. Thurman's ID box. It came from a private residence in South County. The phone is listed with Southwestern Bell under the name of George Belmont."

"That's great! So now you can go pick him up?"

"No, Gil, we can't do that."

Claire couldn't believe what she had just heard, and she asked, "Why can't you?"

Holliday hesitated a moment, surprised to hear her voice. "Mrs. Hunt?"

"Yes, Detective Holliday, I'm on the extension. So, tell me why you can't haul this lunatic in?"

"Well, ma'am, anyone in that house could have used the phone, with or without the owner's knowledge."

"But he admitted he killed three women. You're going to let him get away with that? Without even questioning him?" Gil asked. "And what about his threatening Claire?"

"Who do we question? Some man made a call from a phone at that address. That does not mean he is a killer and that does not mean he even resides in that house."

"So that's it?" Gil asked.

"No, we've made a great deal of progress."

"How do you figure that?" Claire asked.

"We now have a general location where the killer might live or work. We're establishing a stakeout today and will keep an eye on all males coming and going at that residence. We don't want to tip anyone off just yet and give them a chance to change their routine."

"So, other than having a vacation forced on me, and my life threatened in front of thousands of people, we're right back where we started," Claire said, disappointed.

"Don't forget that you're not a suspect anymore, hon," Gil added.

"Very funny."

"Right now, Mrs. Hunt, all you and your husband can do is try not to worry. Let us do our jobs."

"Easier said than done," Gil said.

Claire had heard enough and hung up the phone. She slowly walked toward the front of the store while Gil finished talking with the detective.

When he finally hung up, she asked, "What do you think?"

"Everything he said makes sense. I guess we should do what we're told and stop worrying."

Claire looked at him as if he had just said the dumbest thing she'd ever heard.

IT TURNED OUT to be a busy day at the store. Gil helped customers and rang up quite a few sales. Armed with her love of mysteries and extensive sales experience, even Claire found herself waiting on customers in between dusting and straightening.

Around dinnertime, a young man with long green hair came in. He asked for a book by Andrew Vachss. While Claire searched the shelves, she couldn't help but notice the cup in his hand. It was from the St. Louis Bread Company, just down the street. She could smell the hazelnut blend wafting up through holes in the plastic lid. Without warning, the aroma triggered off a memory she must have been trying to keep buried. After handing the book to the man, she excused herself and ran to where Gil stood.

"Coffee! The GA meeting! Francine! Francine told us about a woman at the meeting. A quiet woman who kept to herself."

"Yes. Her name started with a J. I'm sure of it."

Claire started to run through a list of names: "Jane? Jill? Joan?"

Gil shook his head.

"Jackie, Judith-"

"No...Judy! Definitely Judy! Judy Belmont!"

"You're right. Do you suppose she's related somehow to this George?"

"There's only one way to find out," Gil said.

"No..." Claire whined.

"Sorry, sweetie, but it looks like we're going to another GA meeting."

FORTY

THE HUNTS PARKED across the street from the Congregation of His Almighty Power. They had arrived an hour before the Gamblers Anonymous meeting was scheduled to begin, hoping to catch Francine on her way inside.

"There she is." Gil honked the horn.

"She sure doesn't look very happy to see us," Claire said, waving at the woman.

Francine hurriedly approached them, her head down, hoping the encounter would be brief. The Hunts had seemed nice enough, especially Gil, but she certainly didn't want to be seen with them. Not now. God forbid if they decide to come inside, she thought. Carlos would throw a fit.

"You're not planning on attending, are you?" Francine asked as she stood in the grass by the passenger's side of the car.

"Why don't you get in?" Claire asked, and started to open the door.

"No, I can't."

"What happened?" Gil asked.

Crossing her arms over her chest, Francine talked out of the corner of her mouth. "Delgado. He's furious. Ever since he saw that newspaper story about Claire and the on-air phone call, he goes on and on about how you both came to our meeting under false pretenses."

Claire had almost forgotten the *Post-Dispatch* article. There had also been a report on Channel 5. *Prime Time* had called, wanting to do a segment, but she had refused to talk to anyone.

"Francine, we don't want to upset you. If you can help us with one thing, we'll leave," Claire said, trying to reassure the woman.

"What is it?"

Gil leaned over closer to the window. "Judy Belmont—what is her husband's first name?"

"I think it's Whitey. Yeah, I'm sure of it. Whitey."

"Not George?" Claire asked.

"I told you, it's Whitey. Now I have to go." Francine turned to leave.

Claire called out "Thank you" at the same time as Gil.

Francine waved them off as she walked away.

"So much for that," Claire said. "Now I feel horrible, as if I let her down somehow."

"It's not you," Gil said, starting the car. "They're a tightly knit group and don't appreciate outsiders, that's all. Even if I was a real compulsive gambler, I don't think they would have ever liked me…or you."

"It's not them liking me or not; I can handle that. It's feeling as if I'm contaminated somehow. I feel dirty every time I think about that phone call, that man—those poor women."

Gil pulled onto Highway 40 and kept to his driving, knowing that he had to let his wife talk through her mood.

"Why is this happening? I can't even say 'to me' or 'It's not fair.' I've lived long enough to know nothing's fair, and why should something this horrible *not* happen to me? It's all luck and timing. I guess it's my turn—"

"Our turn," Gil said.

"Our turn for some of the bad. We've had so much of the good. At least since we've been together, huh?"

He smiled. "We sure have."

"Where are we going?" she asked.

"A surprise. I figured we could catch a late lunch, early dinner...whatever you want to call it."

"When Paul was little, he used to say 'linner.'" Claire smiled at the thought of her grown son as a child. She suddenly missed him more than she could convey to Gil.

"Here we are." Gil stopped the car outside of the Botanical Gardens.

"What a nice idea. Thank you, Gil." Claire hugged him tightly.

They got out of the car and walked into the main building. Gil paid for their admissions; then the couple headed for the restaurant. From the cafeteria-style arrangement, they each selected a cold plate and a soft drink; Gil tossed a huge cookie on Claire's tray and winked. While the cashier rang up the last of Gil's order, Gil motioned Claire to grab a table outside.

The late-afternoon sun felt great on her face. She pushed a straw through the lid of her cup and sat back sipping the cold Pepsi while she waited for Gil.

"Now this is nice," he said, clearing a place for his tray on the table. "The roses look great."

"So many colors. I love the statuary by the ponds."

"I knew this would help you relax a bit."

She kissed his cheek.

When they had finished their meal, they decided to walk the grounds, heading toward the Japanese garden.

"Are you feeling better now?" Gil asked.

"I'm fine." She took his hand.

"Then let's talk this through."

"Good idea. Sometimes I think my head's going to explode, everything's getting so complicated."

"Okay," Gil began, "it's been three days since Detective Holliday started watching the Belmont house, and so far he has nothing."

"Right. The Belmont house. Should we just suppose—because I know how much you hate coincidences—that Whitey is George, which makes him Judy Belmont's husband?"

"Yes," Gil said, "we'll start there. Now if we can match Judy Belmont up with each victim, indirectly that would connect George to them, too."

Claire thought a moment, bending over to touch the leaf of a flowering bush. "I like that; it makes sense. So victim number one was Kathleen Sands, right?"

"Right. And we know that she was a waitress who attended Gamblers Anonymous meetings."

"Because Disco King told us," Claire said. "And Judy Belmont attended GA meetings. Victim number two—"

"Mary Dunn, she watched the *Mall* show, loved to go to the boats, and belonged to a shopping club."

"The Shopping Fools," Claire continued, "which may or may not be the same shopping club Judy belongs to but which makes shopping the connection there." She stopped to sit on a bench overlooking a rock garden.

Gil sat down next to Claire. "Which leaves the last victim, Susie Kennedy."

"Whom Millie talked to and met on the boat."

"Two are connected through the boats, two are connected through home shopping, and Judy Belmont can logically be connected to all three," Gil said.

"So, if the killer really is Whitey, remember what he

said to me about seducing women to spend money and buy things they can't afford?'' Claire looked at Gil.

"Yes, and he also said that you made them spend money earned by..."

Together, they finished the thought. "Him."

"Can he really be that crazy to think that his wife is spending all his money and I'm the reason? Would that drive someone to kill innocent people?" Claire asked, puzzled.

"Money is the root of all evil and all that jazz," Gil said.

"Well, it seems to me that it all comes back to finding out if George and Whitey Belmont are the same person."

"You got it," Gil said.

FORTY-ONE

WHITEY BELMONT LOCKED the back door behind him. "Judy? Are you here?" he called out, walking through the kitchen.

No answer came.

Usually, he arrived home from work to find her sprawled out on the sofa. But at least he could keep an eye on her there, make sure she wasn't out gambling. And his dinner was always ready. He wondered if she had snuck away to one of the boats, forgetting he would be coming home an hour earlier today.

The curtains were drawn over the bay window in the front of the house and he pulled back a corner just to check the car again. There appeared to be a man behind the wheel; a woman sat next to him in the passenger seat. They didn't seem to be talking in a particularly friendly way—more businesslike. The woman looked straight ahead. Her severe haircut made him think of Mrs. Jordan, his phys ed teacher from elementary school. Both people drank from white Styrofoam cups. As he released the curtain, Whitey wondered who they were and if he should be afraid.

He opened the door to the hall closet and put his brief-case on the floor inside; then he carefully hung his suit jacket on a hanger. He had removed his tie during the drive home, tucking it into the breast pocket, but now the silky material slid free onto the floor. Bending down to pick it up, he caught sight of several packages shoved in the back of the closet. Whitey recognized the *Home Mall* logo; he would have recognized it from across the street.

Furious, he walked into the bedroom. The walk-in closet was larger than the bedroom he'd occupied when he was a kid. Opening the doors, he reached inside and felt for the light switch. It hadn't made him angry to store his clothes and belongings in the hall closet and guest bedroom. Women had this thing for clothes—everyone knew that—and he had never denied Judy her little pleasures. But he could not—would not—tolerate her lying to him.

Boxes were stacked from floor to ceiling in the far corner, behind her winter clothes. A toaster, two sets of silverware, a food processor, and four complete sets of dishes. Behind him hung silk blouses, wool skirts, at least a dozen dresses, each with a price tag dangling from it.

At first, he was merely angry, but the more he found, the more brand-new pairs of shoes, watches, and cosmetics sealed tightly in untouched packages, the more the rage shook through his body.

"When I'm finished, the only thing left in here will be garbage!" He shouted.

He began with the boxes. Tossing appliances and china against the wall behind their bed, he didn't give a damn where anything landed. His anger only seemed to grow with each item he threw. When everything on the floor of Judy's closet had been cleared out, he stomped into the kitchen, grabbing a pair of scissors from the utility drawer.

At first, he took his time, artfully cutting the sleeve

out of a cashmere sweater or all the buttons off a blazer. He almost started to laugh. But the harder he worked, the more the clothing seemed to multiply, until he was hacking away madly, shouting at every seam and zipper.

JUDY HURRIED INSIDE, still wondering what that dark car was doing over in front of the Richardson house. It had been there when she left for the grocery store and she was sure it had been there when she closed the curtains, around ten o'clock, the night before. She couldn't help but notice the older man behind the wheel; he reminded her of her uncle Phil. She had also noticed Whitey's car parked in the garage. It took her a moment to remember it was the afternoon of his Rotary meeting, when he usually got home early.

"Whitey?" she called as she put two grocery bags on the counter. "Honey, where are you?"

"Get your butt in here!" She heard him shout from the bedroom.

"What's wron—" She couldn't believe her eyes. Clothes and boxes, glass and paper cluttered the bedroom. A spot behind their headboard had several small holes where metal had punctured the drywall. The small lamp, normally on her nightstand, lay smashed.

"This is going to stop right now!" Whitey shouted as he ripped through her new suede coat with the kitchen scissors.

"What is?" she asked meekly, but she knew the answer.

"The excuses, the meetings, the spending—your addictions!" He dropped the coat and stood looking at her. His face was flushed, his mouth contorted like those melting skulls she had seen in a horror movie.

But she didn't back away. "Now, sweetheart—"

"Just look at yourself! You eat too much; you buy too much. You overdo everything, every step of the way. Why is it so hard for you to understand that things should be done in moderation? You never know when to stop. So, my darling wife, I'm stopping things for you."

Tears flooded down her cheeks. He should have known mentioning her weight would make her start.

"Cut the crying; it won't work this time. Look at all this crap! Just look at it!" He grabbed her by the hair and jerked her into the closet.

She tried defending herself. "Most of those things were for Christmas and birthdays. Not for me. I—"

"We don't have one damn credit card we can use. We're being eaten alive. I work my ass off. This is all your fault!"

"But I can't stop. It's a sickness, Whitey. I'm trying to get better, you know that."

He pushed her against the wall; she slumped to the floor, wailing she was sorry. It only made him angrier.

Adrenaline rushed through his body as he went to her dresser and tore open the drawers. Stabbing each article of clothing, he shredded and ripped everything belonging to his wife.

Drying her eyes, Judy got to her feet. She would reason with him. After all, Whitey was a practical man. Coming up behind him, she watched for a moment as he cut into each pair of her panty hose. Then, in the calmest voice she could muster, she said, "I'll get a job. I'll pay off all the bills myself."

He turned, not knowing she was that close to him. The scissors entered her stomach so easily, he was almost as shocked as she was.

Her eyes bugged at the pain. "Oh my God!" she

screamed, pressing her hands to her stomach and falling backward onto the bed. "Oh my god!"

In his other hand, he still gripped half a pair of panty hose, which he shoved into her mouth to keep her quiet.

Why hadn't he thought of doing this sooner? he wondered, looking down at Judy. No, if he had, that bitch Claire Hunt wouldn't have gotten the message. None of them would have.

He pulled the scissors out of the wound and aimed them a little higher this time, closer to her lungs and heart.

She kept saying it over and over until she couldn't say it anymore. "Oh my God! Oh my God!...Oh my G—"

FORTY-TWO

"HOW MANY MORE DAYS are we going to have to sit out here before you realize the guy's clean?" Myra Long-fellow asked her partner.

"The call came from this location," Holliday repeated for the hundredth time.

"It could have been a prank, a nut, but I hardly think that guy we just saw go inside—the geek in the suit—is a killer."

Holliday was ready to argue his side again when a patrol car pulled up, flashing its lights. The two detectives got out of their car and approached the vehicle quickly.

Holding his badge out for inspection, Holliday identified himself and his partner. "So what's the call, Officer?"

"A nine one one—sounds like a domestic disturbance. You didn't hear anything?" the young cop asked.

"No," Holliday said, "but they might be in the back of the house."

"Figures," the cop said, "the call could've come from the neighbors on the other side, over there." He pointed to a yellow house farther down the block from where they all stood.

"We're coming in with you, Officer," Myra Longfellow announced, and started toward the house. The two men followed her.

She poked at the doorbell, anxiously trying to look into the curtained window. When no one answered, she tried the bell again.

The officer opened the screen door and knocked loudly on the front door. "Mrs. Belmont? Open up, please. It's the police."

Thinking that the woman might feel safer opening her door to another woman, Myra Longfellow shouted through the door, "We're here to help you, Mrs. Belmont. Are you all right?"

While the other two waited, Holliday started around the house. "I'll try the back door," he said.

"This sure doesn't feel right," the cop said, and pushed the front door with his shoulder. The chain lock snapped, causing the door to fly open and crash loudly against the wall. "Mrs. Belmont? Mr. Belmont? Police!"

Holliday heard the noise, came back around, and walked through the front door. "There's a window open, looks like a bedroom. Too high for me to see anything."

The uniformed cop pulled his gun and led the way while the three of them walked through the house, checking each room until finally stopping in the doorway of the master bedroom.

"What a mess," Longfellow said.

The cop slowly walked into the room. "Police. Ma'am, are you in here?"

Holliday looked into the large closet. "Someone was definitely very angry here. Look at this." He pointed to the shredded clothing, some of it still clinging to hangers.

Longfellow looked in amazement at the destruction

that must have been going on just a few moments before, all the time she had been sitting right outside in the car.

Careful not to touch anything, the cop walked around the foot of the bed and that was when he saw Judy Belmont's foot.

"Detective Holliday! She's here."

Holliday rushed to where the policeman stood, staring. Bending down, he felt the woman's neck for a pulse. "Too late."

"You mean she's dead?" Longfellow asked. "She can't be."

"Okay, you come check this out while I call in for backup."

Myra knelt down beside Judy Belmont's body and put her ear to the woman's chest, listening for a heartbeat—anything to signify the woman was still alive. But as she looked at the location of the wound and the amount of blood that had been lost, she realized there was no hope.

Holliday took out a paper napkin he had tucked into his pocket after a take-out lunch in the car with Longfellow. He wrapped it around his index finger and dialed the station from a phone in the kitchen.

"That's right, we're at the Belmont house now. Could you check a nine one one call that came in about fifteen minutes ago? Sure, I'll hold."

Longfellow took out a small notepad and started jotting down what they had found and her impressions of the scene, while the sergeant searched through the rest of the house.

"And the call came from what address? Are you sure?" Holliday asked. "Yeah, yeah, I believe you. Thanks."

Holliday knelt down to where his partner sat on the floor. "You're not gonna believe this."

"What?"

"That nine one one call came from here, and it was a man's voice on the tape."

"What did he say?" Longfellow asked.

"He said somebody better come clean up this mess, that he had killed his wife and the Hunt bitch was next."

Longfellow looked at Judy Belmont and then to her partner.

"So what do you think of your geek now?" Holliday couldn't resist asking.

FORTY-THREE

SHE'D BEEN DREAMING of Yorkshire. They were sitting by the fire in the Black Bull, laughing, drinking cider from tall glasses. She felt safe, happier than she could ever remember feeling.

And then the phone rang.

Gil jiggled the bed as he jumped up, hoping it wasn't Allyn calling to say he wouldn't be able to go in early and open the store. Claire knew the chance of getting back to England that day was beyond slim, and she grudgingly got out of bed.

Straightening her paisley nightshirt, she turned on the television, then opened the front door to get the newspaper propped up in front of it. After that, everything started happening at once.

Bold headlines shouted CALL-IN KILLER ON LOOSE.

The local anchorwoman said, "George Belmont, known to his friends and family as Whitey, brutally murdered his wife late yesterday."

And Gil came into the room agitated, yelling above the voice on the television. "That was Detective Holliday on the phone."

Claire pushed the mute button on the remote.

"Well, the first call was him, but just when we were almost finished, another call buzzed in."

She handed him the paper. "And who was that call from?"

"CNN. Can you believe it? Some reporter had the nerve, the goddamn nerve, to ask me how I was feeling about all this? Thank God Holliday had just filled me in."

"What did you tell him—the guy from CNN?"

"I said—and I've waited a long time to say this—'No comment.'"

Claire sat down in front of the television. "Well, I feel like we're standing in the middle of a minefield. Everything's blowing up all around us and there's nothing we can do about any of it."

Gil sat next to her. Together, they listened to the blond anchorwoman finishing up her report on George Belmont. When a commercial came on, Claire turned the set off.

"Did Holliday have anything encouraging to report, or did he just tell you to keep an eye on me?" she asked.

He put his arm around her. "Promise you won't get upset?"

She leaned back to look in his eyes, to see if he was kidding. "I think I'm a little past upset, Gil. I'm working on anger and fear right now."

"Well, you've got to hear this," he began. "There was a nine one one call. That's how they came to find Judy Belmont's body. The caller turned out to be Belmont. He said he had just murdered his wife and that you were next."

Claire couldn't stop the tear that squeezed out of the corner of her right eye.

"Holliday said they did some checking and found that Belmont owns a gun; but they haven't been able to locate it yet."

"Which means he probably has it with him," Claire said.

"Probably. They also found some gun club medals he won, and his records show he was in the marines."

"Which also means he knows how to use the gun and doesn't have to worry about getting that close to me to kill me."

"You have to know all of this, Claire. We can't protect ourselves if we don't know what we're up against."

"I know," she said sadly, "but I have to ask you something."

"Anything, sweetheart."

"Gil, do you think I am responsible in some way for all those women being killed? And Judy? I feel so badly for her."

"No! Don't even think like that. Holliday made it very clear, and he went out of his way to tell me to reassure you that you haven't done anything wrong. A psychologist the police department consults worked up a profile of George Belmont. His report said that all the rage stems from Belmont's inability to live with his wife's addictive behavior. He not only hated her for losing their money but he hated himself more for enabling her. He felt powerless to control his life after awhile. You just happened to be out there—visible—a perfect excuse."

Tears started trickling down her face.

Gil hugged her to him. "Don't go soft on me now."

She pulled away and swiped at the tears with her sleeve. "These are just because I'm so angry."

"Good," he said, "anger can be productive, like getting us something to eat. I'm starving. Or do you want me to make breakfast while you get dressed?"

The phone rang before she could answer him.

Gil didn't move. "Holliday said we should stay in today and he'd call sometime after dinner. I could pull the damn plug on that thing until then."

"Good idea," she said. "Meanwhile, I'll fix breakfast; I need something to do."

WHILE CLAIRE MADE coffee, she thought about Paul. For weeks, she'd been reassuring him that everything was fine. And with him living in Kansas City, there had been some news that she had been able to keep from him. Like the local report about the on-air "killer call." But now with CNN rehashing every half hour how George "Whitey" Belmont had murdered his wife and was probably coming after Claire Hunt next, she needed to be with her son.

"Done," Gil said as he walked in the room and stopped to watch his wife. "I've been thinking."

"Yes?"

"Before Belmont can hurt you, he has to find you."

"True." She poured two glasses of orange juice.

"We're not in the book, no one at the station is about to give out our address, and the bookstore is listed under Old Delmar. We're not talking about a master criminal here; the guy's an average man who just went off the deep end."

"Four times," Claire said. "And he was sure smart enough to find those three women."

"They were all connected to his wife. Friends, or fellow members of some club. It didn't take that much thought."

"So you're trying to convince me that we're safe?"

"I think we're okay as long as we stay here, like Holliday told us to."

"What about visitors, Warden?" Claire asked, setting

the table. "I've been thinking a lot about Paul; I want to call and ask him to take a day off. I miss him, Gil."

The intercom buzzed.

Gil walked to the small box installed in the wall by the front door and depressed a button while he spoke. "Yes?"

"It's the manager, Mr. Hunt. We got a call for you down here in the office. Is there something wrong with your phone?"

"No, we just unplugged it."

"I can't say I blame you, sir, considering everything that's...Well, it's Mrs. Hunt's son. He's worried about his mother and asks you to call him at home."

"Thank you very much; we'll do that."

Claire overheard the conversation from where she stood. Smiling for the first time that day, she said, "We've always had this special—"

"Bond. I know, but it is scary sometimes." Gil started to butter the toast. "Go ahead and call your little boy," he said affectionately, "and tell him I said hi."

FORTY-FOUR

WHITEY BELMONT SAT glaring at the TV. He'd been watching the *Mall* show for hours and Claire Hunt hadn't appeared once, not even in a promo, the bitch.

It had been three days since he'd killed Judy. Looking back at it now, he could see everything so clearly. It hadn't been blind rage; no, Judy herself had forced him to react so violently—and Claire Hunt. Right from the beginning, the two had been coconspirators in a plot to break him financially.

The police had been searching for Whitey ever since he escaped after calling 911. A nice touch, he thought, something to occupy the police who were sitting across the street. He hadn't actually intended to confess on the phone, but the words—and threats against Claire—just came tumbling out.

Now he was hiding out at his girlfriend's apartment, the girlfriend Judy never knew about. He'd been seeing the waitress for over a year, and for most of that time she had been pushing him to get rid of that "fat pig of a wife" of his, so they could be together, forever. He always thought she meant divorce, but apparently she'd been through so many bad times, and bad men, in her life that she meant for him to do whatever it took. Because when Whitey had shown up at her place and told her what he'd done, he was shocked how she'd hugged him, cried out of happiness at the very thought of him doing such a thing for her—for them.

For three days now he had been trying to think of a way to get to Claire Hunt while avoiding the police. He'd taken to pacing around the apartment with the gun tucked into his belt. It scared his girlfriend a bit, but it also excited her. She said she felt like they were Humphrey Bogart and Ida Lupino in *High Sierra*. Whitey didn't think of himself as "Mad Dog" Earle, but then he didn't think of himself as having gone off the deep end, either.

He was holding the gun in his hand, watching the *Mall* show, about five seconds from firing the thing into the TV, à la Elvis, when there was a knock at the door. He got up and went to look through the peephole. The distorted face of a man wearing a brown cap and brown shirt looked back at him. Whitey had seen that uniform before, hundreds of times, whenever the UPS truck pulled up to his house to deliver packages to Judy. He yanked the door open, keeping the hand holding the gun concealed.

"Yeah?"

"Package for—"

"What's that?" Whitey suddenly shouted. He'd spotted the box under the man's arm and saw the all-too-familiar *Home Mall* logo on the side.

"It's a delivery for—hey!"

He didn't get a chance to finish. Whitey grabbed the box, using both hands. The UPS man saw the gun and froze. He'd delivered packages to some crazies in his time, but nobody had ever come to the door with a gun before.

Whitey frantically turned the box around so he could read the label. He thought maybe it was a mistake, just a sick cosmic joke, but there on the label was his girl-friend's name and address. She had obviously ordered something from the *Home Mall*...from Claire.

"Even you," he said under his breath, and then again, louder, "Even you!"

"Uh, look, you don't have to sign..." the UPS man started to say, taking a step back.

Whitey looked at him and a plan suddenly material-ized. Dropping the box to the floor, he pointed the gun at the man. "Get in here."

"Hey, please mister, I'm just—"

Whitey reached out, grabbed the front of the man's shirt, and yanked him into the apartment. He slammed the door, then turned to face the man, who was holding his hands up in front of his face, sinking to his knees.

"Hey, take it easy.... What are ya gonna do?... Aw, man..."

"If you do exactly as I say," Whitey said calmly, "you won't get hurt."

FORTY-FIVE

"WHY DIDN'T YOU tell me how dangerous things were getting?" Paul asked his mother over the phone. "I had to see it on CNN."

Claire got angry all over again, remembering how she had asked her old friend, the station manager at the news channel, to please hold off just a few days. But she was a hot news item now and they had run her story.

"Sweetie, I didn't want you to worry."

"Well, I'm coming there today," Paul said. "I'm going to drive; it shouldn't take me more than three and a half, maybe—"

"Paul, honey, listen to me. Okay?"

There was only the sound of his breathing on the other end.

Claire could well appreciate her son's frustration as she continued to explain. "I want you here; in fact, I was just going to call you. But now I think it wouldn't be such a good idea."

"Why not?"

"Because we have everything under control here."

"Is Gil there, Mom? Can I please talk to him?"

"I am telling you the truth, Paul," she said, a bit indignant. "And, no, Gil isn't here; he's at the store."

"He left you alone?"

"The police are right outside," Claire reassured him.

"Gil has a business to run. We're both trying desperately to have some sort of life here."

"The police are really there?"

"They've been watching this building—day and night—for three days now."

"Jesus, Mom, why is this happening to you?" Suddenly, he sounded like a little boy, and she wanted to hug him.

"Paul, it'll be fine. Everybody gets a crazy person in their life sooner or later. What about that girl you dated last year?"

He laughed. "You mean psycho Sandra?"

"Yeah. Well, this one is mine. The police will catch him, put him away, and that will be the end of it."

Just then, the buzzer by the door sounded, a signal from the doorman.

"Hold on, Paul, I have to get the intercom."

She walked to the door, taking the cordless phone with her.

"Yes?" she said into the white box.

"Uh, Mrs. Hunt? There's uh, a UPS man here with a, uh, package for you."

"All right, Harry," she said, "send him up."

"Yes, ma'am."

She thought Harry sounded a little strange, but how could you tell when the intercom cracked with so much static?

"Paul, I've got to go. The doorman is sending up the UPS man."

"Mom—"

"Don't worry, I'll call you soon." She pressed the off button on the phone.

"Mom, don't let anybody—"

DETECTIVE MYRA LONGFELLOW watched from the un-
marked van across the street as the UPS man double-
parked his truck and went to the door of the building.
He held a brief conversation with the doorman, who then
admitted him. From that point on, she couldn't see either
one of them. She moved away from the window and
looked at the man in the back of the van.

He was the technician for the surveillance equipment,
Detective Al Marino. Marino was in his thirties and not
what Longfellow considered a "real cop." He had been
educated and hired to play with electronic toys. As far
as she was concerned, that did not make him a cop of
any kind.

"I wish I could hear what was going on inside the
apartment," she said aloud.

"Hey, I could have wired it, if you'd wanted," Marino said.

"We needed Mr. and Mrs. Hunt's okay for that, and
they said no."

Marino shrugged. "People want their privacy, even
when they're in danger."

She looked at him, wondering what experience he
could possibly be speaking from.

She turned to watch the TV monitor, noticing how the
UPS truck was blocking their view of the building's
front door. She didn't like it and said so.

"He'll make his delivery and move," Marino said.
"Hey, you wanna get something to eat?"

"I just had breakfast an hour ago."

"I know. Me, too. So, do you wanna?"

"No," she said, "you go."

"You sure? Coffee?"

"Nothing."

"Okay, then. I'll be right back." He slid open the van

door, which was on the sidewalk side, stepped out, and closed it.

She stared at the truck on the TV screen. UPS deliveries were not unusual. There had been others since they'd been on stakeout here. But she didn't remember the driver parking like that before. Maybe it wasn't the regular guy making this delivery.

After about ten minutes, she started to get impatient with Marino. She wanted him to come back so she could go across the street to check things out. The UPS guy had been inside too long. True, he could have had more than one delivery, but when he got out of the truck, she'd seen him carrying only one small box under his arm. Over the past few days, they had recorded every UPS delivery, and it was not unusual for the driver to be inside for a long period of time. A ten-story building, with twelve condos per floor, got deliveries every day—but this man had only one box, so why was he inside for so long?

She went to the driver's side window again, where she had a better view of the front door. From time to time, she'd been able to see the doorman moving inside, but there was no movement now.

"Shhhit," she hissed, "shitshitshit!"

She opened the door hurriedly, jumped out of the van, and sent Marino's lunch flying from his hands.

"Hey!" he said, staggering back from the collision. "What gives?"

"Come on," she shouted. "Something's wrong."

She ran across the street, directly to the UPS truck. She climbed inside. When she saw the trussed-up man in the back, clad only in his T-shirt and boxers, she shouted, "Shit!"

FORTY-SIX

HE ANSWERED THE PHONE on the first ring. "Old Delmar Bookstore."

"Gil, I just talked to Mom," Paul said.

"Your mother's doing fine."

"She hung up on me," Paul interrupted. "She said the doorman was sending up a UPS man."

"Paul, we get deliveries in that building every day."

"She shouldn't be opening the door to anyone. Didn't you tell her that?"

"The police are right in front of the building, Paul."

"But she's still alone inside the apartment. I'm surprised you went to work, Gil."

"Paul," Gil said defensively, "we still have to make a living...." but even as he said it, he felt guilty. It was Claire who had insisted he go to the store and leave her alone.

"I love you dearly," she had said, "but I need some time to myself. I'm feeling smothered by all this."

He'd finally relented and agreed to go to the store. This was the second day he'd done so, and he'd spent most of it the way he'd spent the first, worrying about his wife.

"Paul—"

"I called back, Gil," Paul said, "I called back right away, and there was no answer."

At that moment, a second call made its presence known through a call-waiting beep.

"Hold on, Paul," Gil said, "I have another call. It's probably your mother. Hello?"

"Gil?" It was Holliday.

"What's wrong?"

"We screwed up...royally."

GIL HURRIED HOME after assuring Paul—lying to him—that everything was fine. He parked in front, illegally, near a double-parked UPS truck with a policeman standing near it. The cop tried to stop him, but he rushed for the front door of the building. When he reached it, he saw that the glass of the door had been shattered. The doorman, Harry Wales, was not on duty, but there was a uniformed policeman behind his desk. The other came rushing in behind him. They made Gil produce identification before allowing him into the elevator, but the procedure smacked of closing the barn door after the horse had already cleared the fence.

When Gil reached his apartment, the door was open and several people were inside.

"...had let me install sound equipment this might not have happened," a man was saying.

"I told you," Myra Longfellow said, "we needed an okay for that and—"

"Myra," Holliday cut her off as Gil entered.

"How did this happen?" Gil demanded. "Weren't you right outside the door?"

"Across the street, Gil," Holliday said. "Detectives Marino and Longfellow were in the van across the street. When the UPS truck pulled up, they thought nothing of it. The truck has been here every day since we started surveillance. Sometimes more than once a day."

"And when did you realize something was wrong?"

"The man entered with only one package," Longfellow said, "and he was inside for longer than seemed necessary. I got a bad feeling, so I went to check out the truck. The real UPS guy was tied up in the back. He'd been hit on the head with something, probably a gun."

"Yeah, yeah," Gil said, "I feel real bad for him, but where the hell is my wife?"

"We don't know," Holliday said. "It's obvious she opened the door to Belmont. He must have grabbed her. We checked your underground garage and her car is gone, so he had to have taken her out that way."

"You didn't see her car pull out?" Gil demanded of Longfellow and Marino.

Longfellow opened her mouth to say something, but nothing came out.

"Hey," Marino said, "I just watch the equipment."

Enraged, Gil shouted, "You're supposed to be watching my wife!"

"Not my job, man."

Gil went for him. They would have had to arrest him for assaulting a police office if Holliday hadn't grabbed him.

"Get out of here!" Holliday shouted at Marino.

Marino held both hands in front of him, palms out, shrugged, and left the apartment.

"You, too, Myra."

Again, she looked as if she wanted to say something, but she turned and left. At that point, Holliday released Gil.

All he'd been feeling during the drive over from the store was a cold panic in the pit of his stomach. This rage was something he had never experienced before—

ever—in his life. Claire had been in his life only a few short years, and she had brought him nothing but happiness. If he lost her now, so soon after they'd found each other...

"Where is she, Holliday?" he said weakly, sinking down onto the couch; his legs would no longer support him. "Where is she?"

"We'll find her, Gill," Holliday said. "I swear we'll find her."

"How?" Gill looked up imploringly at the detective. "How?"

Holliday didn't have an answer, yet.

FORTY-SEVEN

CLAIRE HAD BEEN surprised that she didn't feel more fear. From the moment she opened the door and the UPS man had pointed the gun at her, she had known she could die. So why hadn't there been more fear?

"Finally!" the man had said, pushing her into the apartment and slamming the door.

"Who are you? What do you want?" Even as she'd asked these questions, she'd felt as if she were in a bad TV show, reading lines from a hackneyed script.

"It doesn't matter," the man had said.

"You're Belmont...Whitey Belmont. Your wife was Judy."

"My wife," he'd said, shaking his head. "You spoke to her every day."

"I didn't—"

"Oh, maybe you weren't properly introduced, but you knew her all right. And you spoke to her, every day, through the television. You made her buy things, spend money; you preyed on her weaknesses—"

"And that's why you killed her? And those other women?"

Would he react like they did in those bad TV programs? she wondered. Would he tell her?

"Shut up! Just shut up."

"Why should I?" she'd demanded. "I have questions, and if you're going to...to kill me, I have a right—"

A red flush had started creeping down his forehead. "The only rights you have are the ones I give you!" he'd shouted into her face. She'd watched his knuckles turn white as he held the gun on her. Just for that moment, she had flinched, waiting for the shot but still not feeling the degree of fear she had expected.

Whitey had apparently not planned very well. Once he was inside the apartment, he didn't seem to know what to do.

"The police are across the street," she'd said, suddenly seeing a way to distract him. "If you fire your gun in here, they'll be all over you."

"I knew they'd be here," he'd said, "like they were outside my house, but I outsmarted them then and I'm doing it now."

"So what's going to happen?"

"You're going to shut up, and let me think."

She had considered not shutting up, thinking maybe she could rattle him, make him nervous. On the other hand, that might only agitate him more, causing him to pull the trigger. She'd decided to keep quiet and see what he came up with.

"You have a car?" he'd asked.

"Yes."

"Where is it?"

"In the parking lot."

"Outside?"

She'd shaken her head. "Under the building."

"Okay," he'd said, "okay, let's go."

"Where?"

"To your car."

"But I mean...after that. Where do we go?"

"Stop asking so many questions!"

She had felt some panic, but still not fear. At least, she didn't think she felt afraid. She was thinking clearly, and people who were afraid didn't do that, did they?

"We'll get your car. Once we're away from here, I can decide what to do with you."

He'd taken her to the basement garage then, refusing to let her take her purse, which she had reached for out of habit.

"You won't need it," he'd said.

They got in the car and she used her remote to open the gate. As they drove out, she saw the UPS truck, and the police van across the street. She considered ramming the police vehicle with her car.

"If you do anything other than what I tell you," he said, as if reading her mind, "I'll kill you. Turn right." He was sitting in the backseat, right behind her, so she couldn't see him in the rearview mirror.

She turned right, and now they were driving around in what appeared to her to be an aimless fashion. They were on Brentwood Boulevard, approaching the Galleria Mall.

"Where to?" she asked.

"I don't know yet," he said, gesturing with the gun. She caught sight of it briefly in the mirror. "Just drive around—but not in a circle. Just…keep going."

The only thing she could think of was to stay on main streets, so the police could locate them. She came to Clayton Road and made a right. She'd take that all the way through to Lindbergh, if he would let her, and then she'd make a left on Lindbergh and take that through Kirkwood, or maybe get on Manchester….

FORTY-EIGHT

VERY SLOWLY, Holliday explained everything to Gil about what had led up to this moment. How Longfellow had acted on her instincts-not soon enough, Gil thought; how she had run to the front of the building, only to find the doorman unconscious and blocking the entrance. He described how she'd had to smash the glass door to get inside. Finally, how they'd found the apartment door open, and then checked the garage, only to discover Claire's car was gone.

"Where's Harry now?" Gil asked, feeling calmer.

"He was taken to the hospital with a pretty deep gash on his head."

"Too bad." Gil wasn't in the mood to feel sorry for the man who had let Whitey Belmont into the building. Wait until Christmas, he thought.

"Tell me something, Holliday."

"What?"

"Why didn't he just kill her here?"

"I don't know, Gil," Holliday said, "but we can be glad he didn't. Obviously, he's got something planned. And the more elaborate his plan is, the longer it takes him to put it into effect, the better chance we have of catching him."

"What have you done so far?"

"Well, we put the description of your wife, her car,

and the license plate number out on the air. We got the plate number from her registration, which we found in her purse.''

Gil looked around at the mention of Claire's purse and saw it on the dining room table. She never went anywhere without it.

"Hope you don't mind us going through—''

"Don't be stupid," Gil snapped, "I want you to do everything you can." Immediately, he added, "Sorry."

"Forget it. The other thing we can be thankful for is that there's no sign of a struggle. Apparently, your wife played it very smart and went along with him."

"She's a smart girl."

"Yes, she is. How do you think she'll be reacting now?" Holliday asked.

Gil thought a moment. "Calmly."

"She won't panic?"

"No, I don't think so."

"Good," Holliday said. "Then she won't push him into doing anything before he's ready."

"I don't understand," Gil said, "how can you possibly find them? I mean, who knows what's going on in this lunatic's head? He's killed four women, including his own wife. He's a goddamned psycho!"

"Gil…Claire needs you to be calm, too."

"I know, I know," Gil said, putting his head in his hands. "It's just that if anything happens to her…"

Holliday patted Gil's shoulder. "Believe me, we're doing everything we can. Somebody will spot that car."

"Jesus, her car…" Gil said.

"What about it?"

He looked at Holliday. "Do you know how many of them we see in one day? And in that same shade of blue?"

"We've got the license plate number. We'll find her."

"Yeah," Gil said, "but will you find her in time?"

Holliday didn't have an answer for that one.

"And what if he doesn't have a plan?" Gil asked.

"He had to have—"

"No, what if he came up here, grabbed her, and then didn't know what to do?"

"So you're saying they might just be driving around aimlessly?"

"Why not? Is this Whitey Belmont some kind of career criminal?"

"No," Holliday said, "he's got no priors at all. He's been at the same job for years and seemed like a pretty normal guy—until he started killing."

Before Gil could say anything else, Longfellow came rushing in.

"It just came over the radio," she said. "They've spotted the car."

"Where?" Holliday asked.

"Right now they're on Brentwood."

"Doing what?"

She shrugged. "The word we got is that they just seem to be driving around. Come on, we gotta go."

"I'll call you as soon as I know something, Gil," Holliday said.

"Uh-uh. I'm coming with you."

Holliday hesitated just a moment, then decided not to argue. "Okay, come on, then."

FORTY-NINE

CLAIRE COULD FEEL her hands sweating as she gripped the steering wheel. She resented the complete control Whitey Belmont had exerted over her life the past weeks, and especially now. If she was going to die, at least she would do it talking, calmly, instead of pleading or crying.

"Come on, Whitey," she said, "talk to me."

"Don't call me that," he said. He was slumped down in the backseat, looking out the window. "I hate that name. Judy always called me that."

"Sorry. What do you want to be called?"

"My name," he said. "George. My girlfriend, she calls me George."

"You have a girlfriend?"

"Aw, does that offend the perfect Claire Hunt? I've killed three women, plus my devoted wife, and the fact that I have a girlfriend offends you?"

"No, I'm not offen—"

"If you were a man and married to Judy, you'd have a girlfriend, too, just to survive."

"I believe you, Whi—George."

There was a moment of hesitation before he spoke again.

"Got your attention now, don't I?"

"What?"

"You and all the rest of the idiots out there are finally starting to see the real problem."

"Which is?" Claire asked.

"We're a nation of giant sponges," he ranted. "We eat too much, buy too much; all of a sudden, we're this 'Big Gulp' supersized society. There isn't one house out there with just *one* phone or *one* television set inside. Kids have to have their own extensions or it's almost considered cruel and unusual punishment. The old farts, guys who can't even walk gotta have a car—it's their right! And it can't be just any car. No, it has to be a big one so the blind bat won't hurt himself too much when he runs into something. Someone had to start somewhere...to stop it."

"So you started with Kathleen Sands?"

"Give the girl a gold star!" he shouted sarcastically.

"But when the papers got all over the story and started implicating me, you should have been happy," Claire pointed out. "Why did you have to kill Susie Kennedy?"

"They just weren't getting it. No one was! The message I was trying to send got all lost in your publicity. But now, I've got you and if I can..." As if suddenly remembering where he was, he asked, "Where are we?"

"We just turned right onto Clayton. We're driving through Ladue."

"Why?"

"Because you told me to drive where I wanted, and I like the big homes here."

"Big homes," he repeated, "rich people. You know, I work for these people."

"You do?"

"I make decent money, too, but I ended up with a woman who could spend it faster than I could make it.

Her and her friends—sponges—soaking up all the money, all the effort, taking, taking. And it all leads back to you. Isn't that ironic?''

Claire didn't see the irony of it just then. Maybe she would later. But now she had him talking. She took that as a good sign that he wouldn't shoot her…at least for a while.

"ALL RIGHT, GIL, you're here so earn your keep," Holliday said. They were in his car. Longfellow sat next to him; Gil was in the back.

"How do I do that?"

"They turned right on Clayton Road. What will she do when she gets to Lindbergh?"

"What makes you think—"

"The report we have is that she's driving the vehicle. If Belmont doesn't have any kind of plan, then he doesn't know where he wants to go. That puts Claire in charge until he comes up with something. So which way will she go when she gets to Lindbergh?"

Gil closed his eyes and flashed on Kirkwood.

"What?"

"If she has a choice, she'll make a left on Lindbergh and take it through Kirkwood."

Holliday got on the radio and started organizing cars. He wanted one at the corner of Manchester, where Lindbergh became Kirkwood Road. He wanted one in the center of Kirkwood, near the train station, and he wanted one on Big Bend, just before Kirkwood Road got to Highway 44.

"What happens if they get on Forty-four?" Longfellow asked.

"We'll cross that bridge when we come to it," Holliday said. "Right now we need a shortcut to Kirkwood."

"Go to Big Bend," Gil said immediately. "Take it right to Kirkwood."

"Big Bend."

They were on Brentwood, approaching Manchester.

"Make a left," he said. "Manchester will take you to Big Bend, and then you make a right. If they're going to end up in Kirkwood, they're doing it in a roundabout way. We can get there first...if you've got a siren in this thing."

"I've got a siren," Holliday said, "and a bubble. Don't worry, we'll get there."

He produced a red light, which he stuck out the window and affixed to the top of the car. Then he turned on the siren.

CLAIRE MAINTAINED her concentration while trying desperately to send Gil a message mentally.

"Where are we now?"

She tried stalling. "I'm not sure. There's Manchester. I think we're coming to Kirkwood."

"The city or the street? How stupid is that to change the name of Lindbergh to Kirkwood just while you're inside their precious city limits. Don't get on Manchester," he growled. "I *hate* Manchester. It's always crowded with assholes driving vans or pickup trucks."

"I know what you mean," she said.

"I mean, *women* driving pickup trucks, they're the worst!"

"Not worse than van ladies," Claire said. "I hate van ladies."

She couldn't believe it, but she was starting to form a rapport with her captor. According to psychologists, the next thing she'd do was fall in love with him. Yeah, right.

FIFTY

GIL AND LONGFELLOW arrived at Lindbergh and 44 and took refuge in the Steak 'n Shake parking lot. Holliday got on the radio, making contact with the Kirkwood police car situated at Big Bend, hidden behind a gas station.

"Any sign of them yet?"

"No, sir," came the reply. "No sign."

He checked in with the car by the Kirkwood train station and got the same answer. Hanging up his radio mike, he turned in his seat to look at Gil.

"We beat 'em, unless they turned off."

"What do we do when they get here?" Gil asked.

"We'll fall in behind them. We should be able to do that without arousing suspicion."

"And then?"

"And then we'll follow them until we can make a move."

"What if he spots us?"

"Then he'll have to make a deal."

"Why? He's got Claire."

"Let's just…play this by ear for now, Gil. The first thing you want to do is spot them and see that she's okay, am I right?"

"You're definitely right."

"Okay, then," Holliday said, turning in his seat to face forward, "we sit tight."

"But how can we see them from here? What if they get on Forty-four?"

"The car on the other side will let us know. If they take Forty-four downtown, the exit is on our side. We'll see them. If they keep going south, they have to drive right by us and we'll see them."

"If Claire has the choice, they'll head downtown."

"How do you know all this?" Longfellow asked. She turned and looked at him, a puzzled frown on her face. "How'd you know she'd go through Kirkwood, and what makes you think she'll go downtown?"

"When I fell in love with her, Detective, I was determined to learn everything about Claire. She felt the same about me. It didn't take long before we each knew how the other thinks. We can even—"

"What?" Longfellow asked, interested. "You what?"

"Well...sometimes we...communicate."

"Come on!" she said.

"Okay, maybe that's the wrong word. But there are many times when we know what the other is thinking."

"I've heard people who are married twenty years say that," Holliday said. "I think it's true." He still faced forward, keeping his eyes on the street.

"But you two have only been married—what?" Longfellow asked. "A few years?"

"Four."

"How can you form that kind of bond in four years?"

"Because," Gil said, "we were ready for it. Everything that's happened to us in our lives prepared us to meet and know each other. When we fell in love, we opened up completely. It's that simple."

Longfellow stared at him a few moments longer, then turned in her seat and faced forward. She probably didn't believe a word of it.

Gil didn't care.

AS THEY WENT THROUGH Kirkwood, Claire noticed the police car parked near the train station. A coincidence? She hoped George Belmont hadn't seen it.

He'd been quiet for so long that she wondered if he'd fallen asleep. Did she dare slow down and jump out?

"What are you doing?" he demanded suddenly.

"What? I'm not doing anything."

"You were slowing down."

"Just for the light."

"Don't even think about jumping out of this car," he warned her. "I'll shoot you before you could even open the door."

"I won't jump."

He poked at the wire-framed glasses that kept sliding down his nose. "Where are we now?"

Had he fallen asleep? Or did he just have a bad sense of direction?

"Kirkwood. We just passed the train station."

"I know that," he said. "We'll be coming up on Forty-four soon."

"Yes, and if we don't take it, we'll end up going through Sunset Hills and maybe as far as South County."

"I don't want to do that."

"We can go west on Forty-four, head out toward Meramec—"

"No, I don't like that, either."

"Downtown, then?" she asked. "Is that where you want to go?"

"Yeah, that's it," he said, "downtown. Head downtown and get off at Eighteenth Street."

She knew if they got off there and turned right on Jefferson, they would be heading into a sparsely populated area. Turning left would take them toward Market Street, where there were more people. Did she dare do that when the time came?

They reached the entrance to Highway 44 and she took the ramp heading east. The steering wheel was getting slick in her hands; butterflies fluttered inside her stomach.

She was finally starting to feel scared.

Gil, where are you?

THEY GOT WORD when the car passed the train station and were ready when it got to the highway.

"There she is!" Gil shouted.

"I see her."

"Well, go!"

"Let them get on the ramp first," Holliday said. "We don't want him to see us."

Once Claire's car cleared the ramp, Holliday pulled out and got on the highway also. He drove into the middle lane and accelerated.

"Get in the left lane," Gil said. "Claire never drives there; she always stays in the middle."

"Why?" Longfellow asked.

"She says the left is only for passing," Gil answered. "People who stay there drive her crazy."

"Like you?" Holliday asked.

"Like me."

"There they are." Longfellow pointed.

Claire and Belmont were about four car lengths ahead of them, in the center lane.

"This is no good," Holliday said. "If we stay in this lane, we'll have to pass them. I'll have to move into the middle, try to keep a car between us."

He steered over without signaling, positioning a Le Baron between them and Claire's car. Abruptly, the Le Baron switched to the right lane, leaving them with no cover.

"He won't notice us," Longfellow said.

"Don't you hate assholes who don't signal?" Holliday grumbled.

FIFTY-ONE

CLAIRE RECOGNIZED Holliday immediately, and then she saw Gil in the backseat. How they had managed to end up behind her, she had no idea, but she was so glad to see them, she almost said something. She had to bite her lip and gulp back her excitement. If she hadn't constantly been looking in the rearview mirror to try to catch a glimpse of Whitey in case he moved, she never would have noticed them.

Suddenly, she found herself worrying about Gil. What if something happened and he got shot? She'd never be able to live with that.

"George, what's going to happen after?"

"After what?"

"After you...kill me. What will you do, then? The police are looking for you. Do you think you can get away?"

"I don't know."

"What about your girlfriend? Will she help you?"

"I guess."

"You don't sound very sure about her."

"She's just something I had on the side," he said, "a waitress I met."

"So you weren't going to leave your wife for her?"

"Hell no. I never even thought about it. Rita likes to think I killed Judy for her. Like it's some big romantic deal. I didn't tell her it started as an accident, and then…''

"Got out of hand?''

"No,'' he said, "and then I realized it was what I *should* do. For me. It wasn't for anybody else but me.''

"So you're not sorry you killed Judy?''

"Jesus, I wish I'd done it sooner.''

"WHAT DO WE do now?'' Gil asked. "How do we stop them?''

"If we try something…drastic,'' Longfellow said, "we might spook him. We just have to be patient now.''

Holliday was on the radio, trying to get the cooperation of city and county police in covering all exits off 44. If Claire's car didn't get off soon, they'd come to the point where 44 became 55, at which time she'd have to decide whether to head north or south.

"What happens when we get to Fifty-five?'' Gil asked. "Can you cover all those exits, too?''

"We can try,'' Holliday said, hanging up the mike. "Does your wife use her signals?''

"Most of the time.''

"Good,'' Holliday said, "then we'll have some warning when they're going to get off.''

Five minutes later, Claire's turn signal started blinking and she moved into the left lane.

"Eighteenth,'' Holliday said, "they're getting off at Eighteenth Street!''

"GET IN THE LEFT LANE,'' Whitey said. "The exit is coming up.''

She obeyed. Suddenly, Whitey shifted to the right and she could see his face in the rearview mirror.

"When we get to Jefferson, turn right. If you don't, I'll kill you."

"But you're going to take me someplace and kill me anyway...."

"Don't make it harder, Mrs. Hunt." It was the first time he'd said her name.

"Claire," she said.

"What?"

"My name is Claire." Maybe if she became more of a person to him, and not a personality, he wouldn't kill her—but he'd killed four women already. What chance did she have?

"Here's Jefferson," Whitey said, bringing his hand up and over the back of her seat so she could see the gun. "Turn right."

She braked at the stop sign, but before she could make a right turn, the passenger's side window was suddenly shattered.

"WHAT'S HAPPENING?" Gil shouted.

They all had seen the figure come running from the abandoned building, approach Claire's car, and swing at the window with a crowbar.

"Car jack!" Holliday said. "Come on."

He screeched the car to a stop several lengths from Claire's car and he and Longfellow jumped out. Gil scrambled out of the backseat and took off after them.

"WHERE'S YOUR DAMN PURSE, lady?" the thief screamed. It was usually right on the seat next to the bitches. Why was this one different?

Claire had small pieces of glass stuck in her hair and sprinkled across her lap. Whitey was confused. He pointed the gun at the kid—eighteen, maybe nineteen years old—whose head was stuck in the window. "Get away! Get outta here!"

"Whatchooo gonna do, shoot me, motherfucker?" the kid demanded. "Shit! I'll jack you—gimme your fuckin' wallet!"

"Get away or I'll kill you!"

"Fuck you!"

Claire released her seat belt and reached for the door handle.

"Hey, wait—" Whitey yelled, grabbing her.

"Help!" Claire shouted.

"Whatchoo, kidnappin' this lady? Man, that's foul!"

"I warned you," Whitey said. Without hesitation, he squeezed the trigger and shot the kid in the face. The amount of blood that sprayed into the car shocked him and he jerked back, releasing his hold on Claire.

SUDDENLY, GIL WAS THERE, pulling her out of the car. Holliday and Longfellow pointed their guns at Whitey from opposite sides of the car.

"Give up, Belmont!" Holliday shouted as Gil pulled Claire to the ground.

Whitey looked from one detective to the other. "All right!" he shouted. "Okay! I give up!"

"Throw the gun out of the car!" Holliday instructed. "Now!"

Whitey did as he was told. After seeing the kid's face explode, he didn't feel like shooting anybody else anyway.

"Are you all right?" Gil asked Claire.

She hugged him, kissed him, and then said, "Where've you been?"

"Right behind you, sweetie," Gil said, "right behind you."

FIFTY-TWO

"TELL ME AGAIN why we're here?" Claire asked

Gil held the door open for her. "To celebrate. You're alive, you got a raise, and all's right with the world—at least our world."

"No," she said, "I mean this particular restaurant."

"Well, it was recommended, in kind of a roundabout way."

Claire looked for the hostess as they stood waiting in front of a small desk. "Oh, yeah, Maureen, your psychic friend."

"Ever since she told me that Kathleen Sands used to work here, I guess I've been curious, wanted to have a look around."

Claire shook her head. "Those poor women. I can't stop thinking about how they all just came together by chance and ended up making friends with poor Judy Belmont."

"Who happened to be married to a crazy, controlling guy like Whitey," Gil added. "Holliday said the guy even recorded the miles on his wife's car before leaving for work every day...just to keep track of how far from home she went."

"No one deserves to live...or die like that," Claire said.

"No, they don't."

A young woman dressed in a black suit greeted the couple, then led them to a small table near the window.

"And you still don't think I contributed to any of those women's problems?"

"Definitely not," Gil said, "and neither does Thurman."

"Him!" Claire picked up her menu. "He's still on my shit list."

"Even after the raise?"

"Yes," she said, "even after that."

Gil smiled. "That's fair. I guess he should have to pay with more than just his money to win back your friendship." He leaned toward her. "So, dear wife, tell me what you'd like to celebrate tonight."

Claire smiled. "I want to drink a toast to how fortunate I've been to be surrounded by so many inept men lately."

Gil's mouth dropped open slightly. "Should I take that personally?"

"When are you going to learn that when I talk about men in general, I never mean you," Claire reassured him. "But just think about it. If Whitey hadn't been such a sloppy criminal, I might have been killed. Then there was that poor kid, trying to steal my purse. If he'd done it right, broken into the driver's side, I could have been really hurt. And then there's...Benjamin Thurman. If he hadn't been such an insensitive, slimy jerk, I wouldn't be able to buy you dinner tonight."

"I hate to admit it, but you do have a point."

"Unfortunately, I do. But now it's a woman I'm concerned with."

Gil picked up his menu. "What woman?"

"Even though Whitey confessed to killing all those women and leaving the tapes behind to implicate me, there's still his girlfriend. After all, she's the one who had a friend in Motor Vehicles who looked us up and gave him our address.''

"Maybe she was just doing it for love?"

"Are you kidding? She was a coconspirator, an accessory. I want her, too."

"You're a hard woman, Claire," Gil said.

"And you love me that way."

"Desperately."

She reached for his hand. "When I saw you in that car behind me, all I could think about was what I would do if Whitey shot you."

"I was thinking the same thing about you."

She squeezed his hand and went back to reading the menu.

"You know," Gil said, "the funniest thing, if there can be anything funny about it all, is that George Belmont turned out to be an accountant, a man who managed other people's money, but he couldn't handle his own."

"Ironic," she said, "that's what he meant in the car when he talked about irony, I guess."

"What else did you two talk about?"

"Van ladies, pickup trucks, his love life."

"Sounds like you hit it off."

"Oh sure, until he was going to shoot me. We did talk about his girlfriend, though. He even mentioned her name once. I remember thinking it sounded familiar."

Gil smiled. "Well, in your line of work and the way our lives have been going lately, we've both met some real doozies. Like that woman at the GA meeting."

A tall woman with a mass of black hair walked toward them. Bracelets clanked on her arms as she adjusted her shiny belt.

Claire stared down at the table, straining to remember. "It started with an *R*. That woman with all the jewelry, you know. Her name was—"

"Hi, I'll be your server, my name's—"

"Rita!" Gil and Claire said in unison.

"That's right," Rita said in a friendly tone—before realizing who her customers were.

DESERT

BETTY WEBB

NOIR

A LENA JONES MYSTERY

Clarice Kobe is found beaten to death and her ex-husband is the prime suspect. Lena Jones thinks there's more to the murder of her neighbor. Knowing Clarice had a darker side, Lena follows her suspicions to a deadly showdown.

Lena's search for Clarice's killer leads her into a depraved world where love and hate are interchangeable. As she closes in on a killer, she will be forced to make a final choice between acceptance and fear, between life and death, between leaving this world...or embracing it.

"A must read for any fan of the modern female PI novel."
—Publishers Weekly

Available October 2003 at your favorite retail outlet.

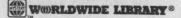